FOREST

The forest is earth and leaves,
sun and shade, feather and blood and bone.

It is the old way, the true way,
the wild way to live.

But, for Kian, wilderness is not home.

Also by Sonya Hartnett

Trouble All the Way
Sparkle and Nightflower
The Glass House
Wilful Blue
Sleeping Dogs
The Devil Latch
Black Foxes
Princes
All My Dangerous Friends
Stripes of the Sidestep Wolf
Thursday's Child

FOREST

SONYA HARTNETT

VIKING

Viking
Penguin Books Australia Ltd
487 Maroondah Highway, PO Box 257
Ringwood, Victoria 3134, Australia
Penguin Books Ltd
Harmondsworth, Middlesex, England
Penguin Putnam Inc.
375 Hudson Street, New York, New York 10014, USA
Penguin Books Canada Limited
10 Alcorn Avenue, Toronto, Ontario, Canada, M4V 3B2
Penguin Books (NZ) Ltd
Cnr Rosedale and Airborne Roads, Albany, Auckland, New Zealand
Penguin Books (South Africa) (Pty) Ltd
5 Watkins Street, Denver Ext 4, 2094, South Africa
Penguin Books India (P) Ltd
11, Community Centre, Panchsheel Park, New Delhi 110 017, India

First published by Penguin Books Australia, 2001

10 9 8 7 6 5 4 3 2 1

Front cover image by Camera Press/Austral
Back cover photograph by Getty Images
Typeset in Centaur MT 12.5/17 by Midland Typesetters, Maryborough, Victoria
Made and printed in Australia by Australian Print Group, Maryborough, Victoria

National Library of Australia
Cataloguing-in-Publication data:

Hartnett, Sonya, 1968– .
Forest

ISBN 0 670 89920 8

I. Title

A823.3

www.penguin.com.au

This project has been assisted by the Commonwealth Government through the Australia Council, its arts funding and advisory body.

Cats, no less liquid than their shadows,
Offer no angles to the wind.

– A. S. J. Tessimond

For Greg,
who loves cats

Contents

The Marble Sky

INSIDE THE BOX they crouched, too frightened to make a sound. Through their feet they could feel they were flying; even in blackness they sensed the speeding hills and trees. They heard the roar of the wind beyond the weighted lid of the box, heard the crank and thrash of the engine and the spin of the tyres on the road. They closed their eyes as though darkness were a dazzling thing, bowed their heads as if the noise, every moment of it come and gone in a slick, slashing instant, was more than their sensitive ears could bear. Above the locked-in odour of each other they could smell smoke, grease, and oil; the box itself tanged with the sugary scent of citrus. The eldest of them, his chest soaked by nervousness, could not hunch into any smaller shape and so waited, frozen tensely to his place; the siblings, still kittens, buried themselves against him for the comfort of hearing his heart. When they felt the car's slowing their eyes flashed open, black and full of alarm; beneath the wheels they heard gravel crunch and grinding, stones pressed together by the burden of the vehicle just as they themselves had been, huddled inside the box.

When the container was lifted they slid forward, grappling at the cardboard. The walls of the box were waxy and high but through them the cats smelled crisp air and huge open spaces beyond. They hit the ground heavily and the lid was pulled back and the animals found themselves blinking at the early stars, at the marbled grey evening sky. The littlest kitten bounded to the lip of the box and was over it and gone, claws scarring the wax. Their confines made vast by her absence, the two remaining cats shrank into a corner. The box was tilted and roughly shaken, and their paws, outstretched, found nothing to catch: the cats sprawled across the muddy earth and the coal-black male kitten darted into the cover of some pampas, his ears sleeked to his skull. The bigger cat stayed where it had landed, flinching in the grass. Through midnight eyes it watched the man, looming tall above. The man gave off smoke, sweat, and the snaky smell of unwashed skin. The man and the animal stared at one another, but the cat made no move: 'Get,' the man said finally, and shoved the creature with his boot. 'Get.'

The cat quailed, blinking, but did not run. The man swayed backward, defied. The cat turned its eyes and, for a moment, denied the very existence of its foe. Then the man reached out and gripped it by the scruff, dragging the animal to him. The cat's mouth came open and it stiffened, claws scything the dirt. The man's hand fumbled under the cat's chin and among the twists of hair, seeking the vulnerable throat. The cat wrenched its hind legs up and they threshed at nothing, its forelegs flailing wildly, but from its gaping mouth came no noise. The man hissed and snarled, forcing the animal's head upward, blinding it with a palm. The cat felt squirming fingers at its throat and then a sharp jerk that severed the cold flow of the air – and suddenly it was free again, dumped forcefully to the ground. It gathered itself against the earth and gazed at the man, who crumpled the animal's collar and threw it aside, the disc and bell jinkling as they fell into the weeds. He stamped a foot and the cat cowered, squinting, groaning. 'Get!' the man bellowed; he snatched abruptly for the creature, hoisting it by the armpits and flinging it as far as he could. The cat dived gracefully, dancing sideways through the grass with its eyes fixed on the man. 'Get!' the man barked, kicking the box so it bucked, all angles, into the air. 'Get! Scat! Get!'

The cat could feel the heat pouring from the man, could smell the bitter mix of frustration and rage. It stayed still as it watched the man bundle himself into the car and the car itself, then, leap into eager life, spinning its wheels as if bursting with impatience to be gone; it raced out of a cloud of its own fumes, gravel stinging off its underside. The dusty pall it left behind hung in the air for a long while, powdering red the dull slate sky.

The pampas whispered as the hidden kitten rose to his feet. The bigger cat shook himself, noting at once the oddness left by the missing collar. Somewhere in his pedigree was a long-haired splendidness of coat that had passed down to him diluted into wispiness, and his ruff preserved a flattened ring: he had worn his collar every day of his five and a half years. As the kitten stepped forward, lifting his paws high from the clammy ground, the older cat sank to his haunches, wanly terrified. He stared at a world that was not his, furling his ears against its peculiar smell and sound. Something bumped his paw and he scrambled back but it was only a moth stuttering a path across the dirt, wings folded primly over stern. The black-and-white cat sagged into the grass, his heart battering.

The kitten, however, was quickly forgetting he had ever been afraid. He stretched his legs and yawned hugely – the journey in the box had been long and cramped. The car still droned on the edge of his hearing but it was a long way off now, and easily ignored. The young cat's coat was jet and glossless and he moved like a shade, gliding past the box and then the collar before trotting onto the shoulder of the road and stopping, on its crest, to look about. On either side of the road was a tract of wet, weedy, liverwort-smeared land and beyond this was wilderness, a jungle of brake and fallen bark and embankments of rotting leaves. Rising out of and above this were the peeling trunks of a forest of ashen trees, the canopy a craggy scribble against the sky. Shadows and darkness concealed its depths mysteriously; the dusk's light glazed the peaks of huge ferns and raffish weeds. The kitten had never seen anything like it, and he walked in circles of wonder. A scarf of darkness slipped between the branches and flapped silently into the clouds and the kitten watched it intently, his golden eyes swivelling in his skull. 'Kian,' he said, 'what's that?'

The black-and-white cat hardly dared glance up. 'A bat. Jem, come here.'

In response Jem feigned deafness, and stayed on the road; Kian continued to scan the scrub, wide-eyed with shock and fear. He had never seen a forest, but some ancestral memory assured him that the crowding of trees with its serrated scents made up that thing, a forest. Kian had been born and raised a suburban cat, and his life, until this evening, had been lived amid glass and brick and steel. He had known a garden with fruiting plants, lawns crossed by stepping-stones, flowers staked neatly in terracotta pots. A forest was not something he had ever even dreamed of, and though his ancestors might recognise it Kian knew with certainty that a forest was not his home. He stared about in dismay, whiskers quivering, coat rumpled by the strengthening breeze, and from the corner of a lime eye he spied a gauzy shadow winnowing between the eucalypts and knew it wasn't an animal or a phantom but the very eyes of the forest itself, staring back at him. His blood ran cold but he made no move, too desolate to flee: this cataclysmic day had shredded his courage and dignity, stripping him of all desire to even breathe any more.

The cold evening silence was rattled, suddenly, as a tiny wagtail, evidently pushed to the brink of its tolerance, nose-dived from the canopy chitting furiously as it came. It rushed for Jem, its minute pied frame spearing the air. Jem ducked as it swooped him, his whiskers blown by the slipstream. The wagtail wheeled and dived again, a flurry of feather and sickle claw, and Jem went prostrate to the road, yowling unhappily. Kian watched as the little bird landed beside the kitten and hopped about in the dirt, boiling with an anger it could not give voice to fast enough. 'Grr grr!' it spluttered at the kitten. 'Meiow meiow! Cak cak! Wa wa! Aargh! Aaargh! Aaaargh!'

The wagtail clearly believed that this gabble, though nonsensical to itself, made perfect sense to a cat: when the kitten did not react as desired, emotion overcame the bird and it leapt into the air, shooting like a wasp for Jem's eyes. The kitten sprang to his feet and bolted. He scuttled past Kian, low as a lizard, the wagtail zooming through the air behind him, and plunged blindly into the forest. The bird alighted on a broken twig and shouted insults after him before fluffing its feathers dismissively and turning its beady glare on Kian. 'Mew,' it told the astonished cat. 'Hiss hiss hiss, mew.'

All birds abhor cats but Kian had rarely encountered one so recklessly passionate about the matter; when his gaze swept the canopy, however, he saw it shudder with an equal animosity. Cats, he realised, were known here, and creatures hated them. He could not stay among the weeds forever so he stepped cautiously into the concealment of the forest and the wagtail supervised his leaving, tail bobbing, muttering abuse. Jem hurried from the shadows and as the two cats wove into the forest the kitten watched the older cat's ears turning and shifting, saw the ivory threads of his whiskers tremble and felt the wariness in each snowy paw, and the last of his bravery deserted him, and he slunk along the earth.

Kian stopped at the base of a stringybark and Jem followed his gaze up its crusted, blood-dark trunk. 'Cally,' Kian murmured, and without hesitation the small kitten came down, rump-first and wriggling, slipping at the last moment so she dropped into a hill of sodden leaves. She stood up and shook herself before touching her nose to Jem's. Siblings, the kittens could hardly have been less alike, for dainty Cally carried no suggestion of her robust brother's sooty hide – instead, her coat was a patchwork of red, apricot, storm-grey and cream, each colour leaking into the others like water in overflowed puddles. Just the tip of her muzzle was white, as if she'd drunk too greedily from a plate of milk, and perhaps walked through it as well, for her paws were similarly stained. Her amber eyes were round, now, and her ears pirouetted. She crouched beside her brother and looked uncertainly at Kian. 'What is this place?' she asked him. 'Why have we come here?'

It went against his feline nature to admit to being nonplussed, so Kian disregarded the question. Jem pinned down a leaf that was ticking in the wind and told his sister, 'The man took off Kian's collar.'

It sounded ominous, and Cally pressed to the ground. Pinging and clicking all around them were the eerie sounds of the shifting forest, the retreat of the daytime inhabitants to secure sleeping-places, the waking of those who rose with the moon. Bickering broke out among roosting birds and the brief flurried commotion was followed by silence fragile as shale. The trees and earth drew breath as one, exhaling a ghost's frosty sigh. The breeze carried an odour that, to the cats, was physical as the trees; streaked as it was with evidence of unknown animals and eccentric landscapes, this spectre of scent was the most nerve-racking aspect of their altogether awful plight. Kian knew he could not strain his senses more vigilantly nor be more prepared to fly, but he felt, and knew the kittens felt, hopelessly endangered and exposed. He stared at the peeling trunks and massing ferns, daunted, fretful for the comfort of his cemented home. 'We don't belong here,' he told the kittens softly. 'We have to go back where we came from.'

The siblings blinked at him: Jem asked, 'Is that place still real? Maybe it's gone. Maybe it's gone – to nothing, and this place is here instead.'

'No.' Kian looked through the canopy to the scattering of stars. 'It's still there, where it was.'

'How do you know?'

Kian paused – he didn't *know* how he knew, yet he felt sure to the core of his heaviest bones, could hear his blood caterwauling that it was true: his home was where it had always been, and it was he who had gone. 'It's there,' he said. 'I promise.'

Cally peered apprehensively into the gloom. Her short existence had been marked by several startling changes, but none so disconcerting as this; she wanted the forest wiped away, her world returned to what it had been. 'But where is it, Kian, that place where it is?'

'How will we find it, Kian?'

Again, the black-and-white cat hesitated. In no direction could he see a landmark, a fence or building or road that he recognised. But twinkling among the early stars were some he had seen before, stars that also shone down on his home, pinpoints that could anchor worlds; through the pads of his paws he could hear the melody he'd heard all his life, the metallic chiming song of the Earth which was sweetest when he was home. A song, the stars: these were things he could track, just as he could put his face to the soil and trace the journey of a worm. He knew he was not wrong in believing as he did, in putting faith in his animal brilliance. 'We can find it,' he said firmly. 'We will.'

'How can we get there?' Cally sat up, interested. 'Will the car take us?'

'No, we'll walk.'

'Is it a long way?'

'It might be. But you have legs, and they'll walk for you.'

Jem jumped up, tail swishing. 'What if we get hungry? Can we eat a bird?'

Cally hedged closer. 'Will it be scary, Kian?'

'Scary?' He scoffed. 'Nothing scares a cat, Cally.'

He hoped he sounded as brave as she needed him to be, as he might genuinely need to be, and possibly quite soon. Within the scrub must lurk a myriad dangers, danger born of the forest and danger at ease in the forest: to trek through it would be to tempt every peril that could befall two small cats and himself, who suddenly felt very small. Kian's life, until this day, had been sedate – he had regularly exchanged hostilities with the loathsome speckled male whose territory neighboured his own, he had decimated the chicks of an enraged and striking myna, and he had once stood his ground in the face of a middling-sized but infuriated canine, the baying of whom had blasted air down his ears; his teeth and claws were keen as thorns, he could ascend any tree, pick a path along any fence, remain serene under the clatter of any truck or train – but much of his five years had been slept away on the padding of a floral armchair. His feline heart, which on countless occasions had assured Kian that he possessed, beside other attributes, supreme cunning, courage and fearsomeness, had nothing to say at this moment, fluttering like a lacewing in a web.

Jem was making plunging attacks on his shoulders and Kian cuffed the youngster, who tumbled in the leaves. Cally was studying him through serious eyes, and reached out a tentative paw. 'Kian,' she said, 'why did the man put us in the box? Why did he leave us here? Why did he take off your collar? And, Kian – where is Ellen?'

The black-and-white cat twinged his whiskers. His gaze drifted to the hair on his chest. Inside the box he had dribbled, frightened, and his hair, drying, had clumped into brittle strings. He groomed these strings, now, with a sudden whole-hearted concentration. He had to crane his neck inelegantly to attend the worst patches and made clumsy work of it, but did not stop until it was done. Then he stepped forward, saying, 'Well then, let's go.'

He ducked through a veil of fern and the kittens scrambled after him, the prospect of becoming separated enough to make them forget the questions left hanging beneath the trees. The last of the twilight was being smothered and soon would roll in true night, the feline's languid ally; in the cats' eyes the pupils pooled and blackened, to capture everything. Over twigs and under branches they slipped, past saplings and rotting tussocks and broken brown seedpods. The forest tracked them as they went, its sunless spirit dodging the trees, pale as a zircon, watchful as an owl. Ears tuned, creeping, tasting air, freezing, guided by stars and a steady magnetic melody rising from the planet's fiery core, the three abandoned cats embarked for home.

Moonlit

THE KITTENS WERE young, and at every turn the world presented to them some beguiling new wonder they had not encountered before. Anything that moved with the faintest suggestion of life – sunshine rippling on a leaf, an undulating rope of caterpillars, a succession of raindrops plipping from a height – captivated their attention with a flawlessness that seemed, to the more world-weary Kian, insane. But the adaptable nature of kittenhood, which expects most things to be perplexing and so recovers quickly from surprise, served Jem and Cally well as they stepped through the forest after Kian. While the older cat was alert to the very curl of his claws, the thoughts of the kittens soon began to wander.

Many things are of grave importance to a feline, and the gravest of them is food. The cats had not eaten since the previous afternoon, and that meal, a sprinkle of dust-dry kibble shaken over the footpath by the man, had been unequally shared, Kian and Jem gulping it down faster than Cally could, and nudging her aside. The calico kitten preferred the days when the old woman had fed them, giving them each a private bowl. Picking her way through spires of native grass the kitten murmured, 'I'm hungry.'

'Me too,' Jem added immediately. 'Kian?'

Kian could sense their hunger on the perimeter of his own but he only glanced at them, and kept walking. With the passing of evening and the arrival of night, the forest had grown quieter. Not purely quiet, for the scrub was crowded with creatures following their moonlit destinies, but the naturally raucous inhabitants – the extrovert birds and rattle-winged insects – were now holding the monastic hushness of rest. Whatever was abroad in the darkness, stalking, repairing, feeding, wooing, preferred to keep its business, if it could, to itself. Nonetheless Kian felt surrounded, and oppressively harried, by squawks and wails of a kind he had never heard, by appalling shrieks that lacerated the icy air, and each that skidded by him left him feeling slightly more shredded than the last. He didn't know what there was worth fearing in the forest, but it sounded hideous.

'Kian?'

'. . . Yes?'

'Did you hear us say we're hungry?'

Kian paused on the crown of a boulder, considering the

stars. They shone brightly across a pearl-grey sky, spiked as summer burrs.

'Kian?'

'What?'

'There's lots of trees here.'

'Hmm.' Through the spongy floor of the forest Kian could feel the guiding song, a drone that vibrated through the pads of his paws. The cats were walking in the furrow of a rodent's trail, and the tips of overhanging fronds splashed Kian's nose with dew. No footstep he took was soundless, however deft he tried to be. At the press of each paw a leaf would fall, a stick would snap, a clod would roll away, and this treacherous trait of the scrub was becoming a torment to him. 'It's a forest, Jem.'

'Yeah, a forest . . . Kian?'

'What?'

'Why are there no street lights?'

'There just aren't. Shh, Jem.'

'It's very dark.' The kitten hopped over a eucalypt's felled limb. 'That's because there's no street lights. You know what else there isn't?'

'Jem, be quiet . . .'

'Cally? You know what else?'

'What?'

'There's no aerials. And you know what else? Kian, you know what –'

'*Quiet!*' Kian wheeled, hissing into the youngster's face. 'I said *be quiet!*'

And then, as if awaiting this chance to disobey, a maniacal scream careened through the forest, stripping as it went the leaves from the trees; fast on its heels raced another, a wraith of rage which sent blackbirds splintering into the air. Kian and the kittens dashed for the shelter of a tree-fern and from beneath the umbrella of fronds they watched a massive piebald cat swoop through the jangling canopy, howling as it came. Its great legs launched it on soaring flights that linked the gum trees and Cally scarcely had time to realise it was coming straight toward her when the mottled giant changed direction – indeed, it threw itself skyward and for an instant was silhouetted against the moon, a twisting, screeching sinew. It landed on the bough of a messmate, nose-to-nose with a cat equally monstrous, tawny-yellow, who slammed a paw so violently into its face that the momentum almost threw the blotched beast from its perch. The dappled cat reared, stunned but boxing viciously, and the tawny animal retreated, reversing agilely along the branch. The piebald jumped after it, mouth agape and swearing, but stopped wisely beyond reach of its adversary's punch. For a burning moment they stared at one another, high up in the canopy, while the woken birds flapped and squawled and a shower of leaves whirlygigged to the forest floor. Beneath the fern the urban cats cringed, chins against the earth. Above them the titans glared, lips hoisted over dagger fangs. A rumble began in the throat of the second and was caught like birdsong by the first, both cats so irate that they smelt vaguely smoky. Neither made a move. Unexpectedly, one spoke: the darker told the lighter, 'Someone's plucked an eye from you already – you're one-eyed at both ends. Why don't you let me scoop out that leftover orb? My claws are just *a-itching*.'

The yellow gladiator sniggered. 'No one took that eye from me, scrote. I ripped it out myself, when I had nothing better to do. Come here, I'll show you how.'

The piebald chortled, his tattered tail slashing. 'You got a smart mouth, you do. Pity your feet aren't so quick, eh?'

'They're not as quick as yours, that's true. You run like the wind. Maybe because you get so much practice.'

The dark fighter narrowed his eyes. 'No need to get nasty, Loke. You'll hurt my feelings.'

'I squirt on your feelings, Whit.'

They had both caught their breath and now, revived, dashed forward on rigid legs. They came growling and gurgling, their terrible teeth bared, and threw themselves with gusto into the clutches of each other. Fangs and claws buried in pelt, they wrestled only an instant before toppling from the limb, falling the distance as a single animal, bound in the arms of the enemy. They rushed to earth like a comet, and Cally, following their descent, glimpsed a small striped cat sitting in a patch of open ground with its chin tilted, watching the fall just as she was doing, realising, as she did, that the plummeting pugilists were about to land on him.

He reacted as if stung by a hive's worth of hornets: he wailed and hurtled sideways, crashing through the fronds and ploughing into the kittens and Kian, who fled chaotically as the warriors hit the dirt. One spotted Kian instantly, spun on its claws and surged after him; the other, dazed by the fall, loped after Jem a moment before pivoting to become the confederate of its erstwhile foe. Like lightning Kian flashed across the clearing, vaulting for the tall messmate. His claws caught the bark and he scrambled frantically at the trunk, his legs extended like a spider's, but under his weight the scrappy bark broke away and he clung futilely to the pieces as he flopped to the ground. He bunched himself against the tree-trunk and blinked at the ferals who stalked relentlessly for him, eyes murderously aglow; from the bramble where she'd hidden Cally saw the first brawler glance at the second, chuffing throatily. 'Looky here!' he cawed. 'Look what hopped out of the scrackle! A shiny little froggy, hoppy hoppy hop! Froggies hopping everywhere, whacky whacky whack!'

The tawny cat, one-eyed Loke, ignored his imaginative friend; he sniffed the air through a battered nose, snaking his head close to Kian's. Kian lay motionless, flat on the dirt, his heart hammering. He could see the sunken socket where the feral's eye had been, a seam of clammy liquid welling along the lid, and smell its rank aura of decay. The wild cat asked quietly, 'And who are you?'

'No one –'

'I know that.'

'My name is Kian –'

'*Key-arn.*' Loke stepped nearer. 'I didn't ask you what your name was.'

'You *suck*, Kian!'

Kian kept his gaze low. 'I don't mean any trouble –'

'But I think you do. I think you want our territory.'

'No –'

'I think you want our food.'

'No, I –'

Loke pulled back sharply. 'You are . . . not-tom.'

'The other one, too,' said Whit. 'The titchy one. Not-tom. The wind blows cold between your pegs, eh, frog?'

'Well,' the blind feral snickered, 'you won't want our pussycats.'

Kian huddled to the messmate, his eyes black as onyx, fighting a hectic instinct to run. 'I'm nothing,' he breathed. 'I'm really nothing.'

'We can see that, not-tom!' Whit leered down at the lost cat, his mottled coat shedding fur. 'You're nothing but nothing but nothing! Look at you, pretty, with your shiny white belly and paws. So clean and fluffy and sweet. They've never been splashed with the red, have they? Never with the gushing hot red. Is that where you come from, not-tom, you and the midget not-tom? Some pretty lovely shiny-cat place, eh?'

Kian felt the eucalypt's rough bark at his ears. 'We come from somewhere far away – a man put us in a box in a car, you see, and he took off my collar and left us here, and –'

'Shut it, rag, we don't care!' The feral threw a brutal punch, gashing Kian across the nose. 'We're not interested, understand? You're here now, where you're not supposed to be! No more hopping for you, frog!'

Whit's cavernous mouth opened and he hissed into the urban cat's eyes a blare of rancid air. Every animal instinct told Kian to strike back or flee: instead he tucked himself up tighter, quaking dramatically, pathetically subdued. The ferals, expecting something livelier, stared at him suspiciously. 'What's wrong with Shiny?' Whit snapped. 'Why doesn't he move?'

Loke rapped Kian's head and the refugee moaned; Cally, in the bramble, trembled miserably. She could see Jem peeking through a clutter of gum leaves, two rings of gold betraying his eyes. Whit, baffled by the victim's lethargy, lowered his brandished paw. 'Get up, scrote!' he shouted impatiently. 'Fight! Run!'

'Why should I?' Kian sighed, blood dribbling down his nose. 'What's the point? I couldn't escape from you.'

'That's right, you couldn't!'

'So why try?'

Loke snorted, flicking a scurfy tail. 'Shiny's trying to trick you, Whit. He knows you're an idiot.'

The piebald feral bristled. 'I'm a lover and a feuder and a slayer – I'll show Shiny who's idiot!'

Kian scrambled as the brawler lunged for him, the feral's paw thumping the air. Reversing into the cover of grass he cried, 'It wasn't *me* who said that!'

The attacking warrior paused, his tail drooping to the ground. His gaze slid slowly sideways and fixed itself on Loke. 'The cat who called me idiot was one-eyed.'

'Oh, shut up, Whit!'

'Shut up yourself, Loke! You're not so clever!'

'And you're as smart as dogshit!'

Screaming with the insult the blotched feral sprang for the throat of his blinded brother, who defended himself swiftly and without mercy. Beads of blood splattered the clearing and Whit staggered into the darkness, his jaw slung with pain. Loke rubbed his frowzy head, patting down a flap of skin; his empty socket dripping fluid, he turned to Kian. 'Get lost, not-tom,' he spat. 'You puny coward.'

Kian got to his feet, and crept from the grass with prudent care. The tips of his whiskers brushed the flanks of the fighting cat as Loke leaned close to whisper; though he kept his ears submissively folded, Kian heard every word.

'Some cat in this forest is gonna shred you,' the feral told him. 'Won't be me, though. Mewler like you would be mud on my reputation.'

Kian said nothing but trod away steadily, heedless to the direction he chose. He did not halt or even glance behind when he heard the litter rustle and knew the brawlers had vanished in the night. He kept his pace calm, his tail slack and his head down. Apart from a smarting nose he was unhurt and thus triumphant but inside himself he choked on humiliation, wounded to the core by the crime he had committed against his proud but fragile feline self.

The Spleenwort Stream

JEM SLITHERED DOWN the eucalypt and scampered through the undergrowth after Kian, desperate not to become lost in the forest. He could hear his sister running ahead of him and they met a moment later, as Cally slowed at the sight of the bigger cat. Kian had his ears turned, listening to them, but he did not look around to see them struggling in his footsteps. He shook his feathery ruff and coughed, clearing his throat.

'I know you're hungry, kittens, and I know you're getting tired. But this place isn't safe for us, and while it's night we need to stay awake and watching. In the morning you can rest, and I'll find you something to eat. You'll be all right until then, I think.'

Jem hurried alongside him, touching his brow on the older cat's chin. In truth he had forgotten feeling hungry and he doubted he could ever sleep again, so giddily thrilling had the feral encounter been for him – he'd feared his eyes might spring from his head, so ravenously had he watched. Jem had never been in a battle and the few he'd witnessed had been comparatively tame affairs, conducted between cats unwilling to come to serious grips with each other: in his young heart dawned, now, the longing to become a ruthless fireball of a feline, an awesome equal to the warriors he had just seen. The brawl and the forest and the journey in the car had made this, for the kitten, a most intoxicating day, and Jem would have sworn that nothing had the power to startle him again that night – until the striped cat materialised without warning and the unexpected apparition sent the kitten bounding into the air, electrified with fright.

Kian, however, was in no mood for further cowardice: in a flicker he assessed the strengths of the stranger and, judging himself the better equipped of the two, leapt forward with a barbaric yowl, dealing the tabby a claw-studded blow that sent it tumbling, its tail twirling frenziedly with the loss of equilibrium. Kian pounced on the capsized creature, his weight pinioning it to the dirt, growling gruesomely in its ear. The striped cat did not squirm and when Kian realised he was meeting no resistance, that he was rumbling into the face of a limp pacifist, he jumped away and stood staring, leery and embarrassed, foiled by the very strategy he had employed on Whit and Loke.

The tabby got to its feet, snuffling and rubbing its muzzle with a paw. It fussed over repairs to its toilet without glancing at the hackled urban cats, clearly wishing to be presentable before introducing itself. It shook a wodge of muck from its toes, combed its sparse caramel whiskers, and chewed a disquietened flea. It twisted its backbone to reach its rump, where it licked quiffs of disarrayed hair. It was a young cat, cobbily built and snub-nosed, not yet carrying adult muscle or weight; its short coat was banded in copper and coal, the honourable colours of the ancestors which it wore with evident pride. When the restorations were complete the stranger set his paws together and gazed calmly at the bemused refugees. 'My name's Marlo,' he announced. 'I heard what you said back there, about the box and the car. There's someone who wants to meet you.'

'You were in the clearing.' Cally, in the moon-shadow of Kian, glared accusingly at the tabby. 'Those fighting cats nearly squashed you. And then you ran into us.'

The youngster's tail swished peevishly. 'That wasn't my fault. I didn't know you were under the fern. It was your fault, you shouldn't have been there . . . Well, anyway. That's finished now. Come on.'

'Kittens, wait.' Kian looked into the forest, at the strew of vegetation that shambled darkly to the sky. 'Where are you taking us, cat?'

The tabby's stripes rippled. 'Not far.'

The black-and-white cat scanned the scrub mistrustfully, searching for the quartzlike reflection of eyes. He knew he was watched, could feel pinpoints of brilliance prickling his skin. Aloud he said, 'We don't mean any harm. We're trying to go home. These kittens and I will pass through the forest taking no more than we need, and once we're gone you won't hear from us again. We shouldn't be tricked or tormented or attacked or teased . . .'

He petered out; the tabby blinked blandly. 'Come on,' he drawled. 'No one's gonna eat you.'

Kian felt the vigilant eyes and, with a sense of resignation that descends rarely on the feline heart, let the feral show them the way. They followed a silvery tail through thickets where slender mountain ash soared from vibrant beds of fern, the peeling trunks so crowded that a kite could not dip between them with its wings outspread. Cally walked in silence behind Kian, the tuft of his swishing tail like a dandelion brushing her face; Marlo, sauntering in the lead, fell to chatting with Jem. 'What did you think of that brawl?' he asked the kitten. 'Cool, hey? They're mangy and mean, Whit and old Pus-eye, but they're excellent feuders. I watch them all the time.'

'I watched them too, I –'

'Whit's got speed, he's fast as a hawk, but Loke's the smarter one. Did you see him punch? Pow, straight across the gob. Whit never saw it coming. I watch them nearly every night, I know all their moves. One night I'm gonna run up the tree and then *wham!* They won't know what's hit them.'

'And me,' breathed Jem, 'I could fight them too.'

Marlo looked loftily at the kitten. 'Maybe when you're grown.'

The trail had brought the cats to a rocky cleft in the earth, in the shallow basin of which ran a slip of fragrant water so cold that fog lingered over it in meandering coils. The rocks were padded with moss and flakes of fungus, and those that lay beneath the water were slimed with green algae. The banks of the creek sprouted brake and spleenwort, and fishbone fern which bobbed to the water reverently. All about hung a talcy mist that dampened the tips of the cats' ears. Cally crept to the edge of the creek and touched her chin to the water; instantly the slippery bank sent her skidding into the depths where she gasped and floundered, clambering at the air. Kian, Jem and Marlo watched as she was dunked and surfaced spluttering, her eyes huge with terror. Her flailing claws hooked a trunk that bridged the creek and she dragged herself up its flank, water streaming from her hair. Slick as a newborn she scudded along the trunk, an arc of droplets flinging off her as she jumped to mossy earth. Drenched and shivering and separated from her companions by the expanse of ice water, she curled into a leaking ball of woe; Marlo, realising with regret that the spectacle was over, called suddenly and stridently, 'Tey! Here's those cats I was telling you about!'

From the chasm of blackness massed beyond the creek stepped a dun-coloured she-cat on grubby white paws, who stopped beside Cally and licked the worst of the water from the kitten's eyes before glaring at Kian. 'It's not safe for cubs to drink here,' she told him rebukingly. 'It's muddy and steep, can't you see?'

Kian flexed his whiskers, and as his gaze swept the bramble he saw faces, first one and then another, then more cats than he had ever seen collected in any place. In the grainy night the masks of a cat clowder hung, ghostlike, disembodied, cats transformed into whispers or memories, cats like spirits returning home from the valleys of the underworld, all of them watching, waiting, listening to him. To Jem, by his side, Kian muttered, 'Stay down.'

A rough-coated slate-grey male dived from a height and hit the ground behind the she-cat; he pushed through a snag of fishbone and strolled onto the bridge of eucalypt, the water flowing silkily below him. He sniffed the air and tasted it before declaring, 'It's true. Not-toms.'

The hackles rose the length of Kian; Cally lashed for the grey feral when, stepping stylishly from the log, he bent his tousled head to her. He closed his emerald eyes to the strike, saying, 'This one too. She won't have cubs.'

He turned his head to stare at Kian and asked, 'How can you go on?'

A ripple of amusement went from tree to tree, sliding down the veins of dangling leaves. Kian stood to his full height and with blistering dignity hissed, 'Where we come from, many cats are the same as we are. No one mentions it, let alone finds it comical. To do so would be considered unforgivably uncouth.'

This indignant utterance entertained the grey feral mightily, although, as cats are not given to extravagant expressions of hilarity, he merely shut his eyes and appeared to quietly choke. While he was offguard the she-cat cuffed him and he bounced backwards impishly. 'Shyler,' growled another cat, old and pitch as midnight, who lay in a bed of frothing fern and toward whom the untidy male turned, immediately subdued, 'sit.'

The young tom sat, and the nocturnal stillness that followed soon soothed the baleful blood in Kian's veins. The ferals and the refugees considered each other from their opposing sides of the creek as the cold air coasted by them, heavy with the scent of wet earth and gum tree. None of the clowder cats were as large as the warriors, Whit and Loke, had been: Kian saw that the group included kittens and gangly adolescents, the weak and wounded and aged. On the outskirts of the gathering drifted the whiff of males nearing their prime, while the acidic odour of a few mature toms rose solid as a tree from the company's core. The strength of the clowder, however, lay in its females – in the mothers, daughters, sisters and aunts who lived in the vicinity and found in their alliance safety and power, and camaraderie too: Kian saw that these cats gathered for the restful pleasure of being a cat amongst cats.

The forest around the animals remained tranquil; the grey tom Shyler had sunk on his paws and the only sound was of the creek water swelling over the stones, the only movement from the she-cat, Tey, who continued to dry Cally. Tey was small, thin even for her size, and bony in the hips; her loose belly was testimony to years and many litters, and she preened the wet kitten expertly. As she worked, she glanced now and then at Kian. Finally she asked, 'Where is it, this place you say you come from?'

Kian was sitting primly, Jem crouching at his side. 'It's somewhere a long way from here,' he said. 'It's not like this place.'

'What's it like, then?'

The suburban cat paused. It would be wasted effort, attempting to explain the details. Kian had once encountered a mechanical mouse, with wheels on its stomach and whirring insides: describing his civilised world to these wild cats would be as difficult, and as futile, as explaining the toy to the real mouse, who ran on flesh and grain. 'There are houses,' he began lacklustrely, 'one after another in rows. There are roads, and lots of cars. Every yard and building is the territory of some cat or another. Most cats have a human who lives on the territory – ours is called Ellen. She's decrepit, but she's attentive.'

'You're right,' agreed Tey. 'A place like that would be a long way from here. How did you become so lost from it? Is it true, what you told Whit and Loke – was there really a man and a car?'

'There was. A man put us in the box and left us here. I had a collar because of the woman and the house belonging to me, but the man took it off and threw it away.' Kian stopped, and sighed. 'I know it's hard for you to understand –'

'No,' said Tey, 'I understand. I've heard your story before.'

She paced closer to the creek's bank; Cally tottered to her feet and followed, her coat licked greasy and flat. The halo shining in Tey's eyes was the colour of honey and clay.

'My mother used to say she'd once lived in a house,' the she-cat began. 'She said she'd been put into a crate one day, and when the crate opened she found herself here. She would talk about that first night in the forest, how frightened she had been, how she could not believe in the forest and wondered if she'd stopped breathing without knowing it. She used to tell me about her other life, about sapiens and gardens and cars. I didn't believe her, when she said these things, I thought she must be mad. I thought she had imagined it . . . yet here you are, and the story is the same.'

Jem and Cally looked at Kian, who asked, 'Where is your mother? Maybe, if I could talk to her –'

'She isn't here.'

'She went back? She found her house?'

Tey blinked impassively, settling on a stone. 'My mother has melted into the soil, as all cats must do. She was a poor hunter, she could hardly finish off a cicada; she was always trailing kittens, who sucked the strength from her. She was only bones and scruffiness, harassed each time she lay down. Her life was spent moving – she ran and ran and ran.'

'She was searching for home –'

'No.' Tey's tail switched. 'I don't say so. She was only running. She had no home to search for – she was lost, you see. She was the most lost cat ever kindled. I'm glad, for her, that she doesn't have to breathe any more.'

The black tom spoke gravely. 'Life is hard, for a cat who loses a house. Better never to have had one at all.'

Cally, unnerved, left the she-cat's side and crossed the prone tree-trunk, watched as she went by Marlo, who longed to push her off. She reached the far bank and hurried to her brother; both kittens, then, gazed searchingly at Kian. The black-and-white cat was rattled by Tey's story, and groomed his face and whiskers until he felt tolerably calm. He looked across the creek then, and told the clowder cats, 'I will get home.'

'Perhaps you're not supposed to.' The black tom stood, arching and stretching his spine, and Kian saw that he was gaunt, his eyes sunken, that he wasted beneath some deathly disease. 'Perhaps fate brought you here, and perhaps it doesn't mean you to leave. Perhaps this is your destiny, here, with us.'

'No.' Kian set his teeth. A cat believes in fate only when no other option exists, when it lacks the ability to change anything and must make do with what it's been given, and Kian was not ready to accept that defeat. 'I am free to go – I must go. I can feel my home calling me. It's wrong, for me to be here. This is your place, not mine.'

Again there came a ponderous silence as the cats contemplated each other. Several of the clowder had come down from the trees to curl in a bank of hare's-foot fern and tend one another absently. Others sat regally alone, the tips of their tails wagging with habitual irritation. Still others remained on the boughs, scrutinising every distant call, or gliding away like gossamer on missions unexplained. The unkempt grey Shyler scratched an ear with a hind foot and yawned massively; Marlo tucked his paws beneath his chest, to keep them out of trouble. Tey's attention wandered from Kian to the kittens and her smudged paw twitched, craving to drag them closer. Jem pressed against his sister, smelling on her the sourness of Tey's tongue; on the thin raw air skimmed other scents, the bite of the water, the rot of the forest, the earthiness of the wild clowder. The kittens' first winter had almost come and Jem was growing a thicker coat, which felt weighty and ill-fitting but kept him reasonably warm. Fearful he would miss something, he struggled to stay awake, but the heat of his coat, the adventures of the day, the closeness of the clowder and its low placid hum, lulled him irresistibly, and coaxed his eyelids down. Next to him, Cally's head slumped deeper into the cushion of her paws. Tey watched them with the fond concern of a mother; of Kian she asked, 'What will you do about them?'

'They will come with me.' Kian glanced at the sleeping siblings. 'This isn't their home either.'

'They will hamper you.' The black tom's eyes glimmered in the moonlight. 'Can they hunt? Can they fight? Can you do that for them, as well as for yourself?'

Kian faltered. 'I suppose.'

'Don't be absurd. Their company will make you vulnerable. You're risking your life, if you take them with you.'

Kian looked at the kittens, confused. It had not occurred to him to desert them: in his thinking, and lack of it, he was, he knew, a very pampered cat. He turned to the feral tom, whose tail slapped disdainfully. 'They wouldn't survive out here.'

'Why wouldn't they? All of us have done. But their survival isn't your concern – you have a duty to your own life. Walk off, Kian: when they wake, we'll tell them you were just some cat they dreamed.'

Kian looked back at the kittens. Now he thought of it, the prospect of caring for them did trouble him somewhat. He was not convinced he could do so adequately, knowing none of the requirements of guardianship. He was, after all, a male cat, footloose. Something dreadful might befall them simply because he had not the nous to foresee and prevent it. The instinct for self-preservation is not one that sits peacefully inside a cat – it is always searching for ways to better satisfy its single, adamant need - and now it and all his ancestors were pointing out the wisdom in the black tom's words, suggesting Kian would be moronically canine to forsake this opportunity. He lifted his lime eyes and scanned the wild faces, all of them waiting with tense interest for his reply. It was astonishing, to him, that this community of savages should thrive. Back home, on his armchair, he would never have guessed its existence. Many cats, countless cats, all of them living ruthlessly, each dawn renewing the challenge to stay fed, sheltered, alive. He remembered the wagtail and its fevered attack on Jem: what was the reputation of these cats, if the sight of even a kitten should fill a bird with such suicidal rage? Kian stared into the trees: accustomed to tiled roofs and telephone poles, his eyes felt injured by the wilderness they saw. The kittens would not fare well, he knew, adrift in such a bloodstained world. Some cat would kill them for the sheer sake of it.

Tey spoke, and he spun his ears to her. 'If you want,' said the she-cat, 'I will watch them for you.'

He looked at her, trusting and believing her. Tey, he sensed, was a cat of some standing, one given her due respect.

Many of the clowder were her offspring and descendants and if Tey decided that Jem and Cally should not be harmed, these others would uphold the command. The instinct for solitary survival was insinuating itself through every fibre of Kian, suffocating as vine – yet he hesitated. To the she-cat he said, 'They're hungry.'

'I know.'

Kian tightened his jaw. He stepped experimentally away from the kittens. In an instant he felt himself freed, rescued from the weight of their defencelessness. He looked about hastily, uncertain which direction to go, and his eyes touched on Cally, who had woken and squinted blearily at him. She yawned and her wakefulness woke her brother, who stretched himself from whisker to tail. Still half-asleep they stumbled to his side, ready to follow him though wonky on their paws. Kian felt the burden of them resettle on his shoulders, staggering slightly beneath the load. The ferals watched in silence as he tidied Jem's hair. A cat shirks and detests responsibility but in his heart Kian had come to feel that these kittens belonged to him somehow, and a cat also resents losing what it reckons to be its own: at least for the moment he felt quietly pleased. To the ferals he said, 'Maybe this is fate.'

The wild cats looked at each other, and the grey tom Shyler scoffed. 'Maybe you're talking out your craphole,' he said. Tey struck at his nose and he darted through the fishbone. The lean she-cat turned to Kian.

'There's a lizard ground nearby,' she said shortly. 'In the morning, Marlo can show you where. The cubs will get a meal.'

A grizzle of annoyance swung the cats' attention to a dappled female who sat between mossy boulders and who had, until now, followed the conversation without seeming concern. She got to her feet, her tail whipping. 'Those lizards are ours,' she said. 'There's almost none of them left. Cold is coming, Tey – birds will fly, rodents will burrow, the bugs will blow away. All of us will be hungry soon.'

'These kittens are hungry now.'

'They're not your kittens to worry about. It's been a long time since you had kittens of your own. But many of us have cubs – *clowder* cubs – and they all have guts that need filling. It's wrong of you, kittenless Tey, to give away our food.'

Tey's lip curved over pointed teeth. 'I fed you, Bodeyn, and your littermates, when your own dam was taken by the steely cobweb. I fed you and cared for you, though I had kits in the nest. I warmed you and kept you clean. Would you prefer it, if I'd left you to the rats?'

'But I am clowder. We are the same!'

'You are clowder, but show me the rat who'd care!'

Bodeyn, scowling, hedged amongst the rocks. 'I'm only thinking of us, Tey,' she grumbled. 'I'm only thinking of you. Cats like these bring sapiens into the forest, and who ever heard anything good about a sapien? Let them go and find a human, and eat the human's food.'

The black tom pricked his ears. 'There is a house,' he said, 'at the edge of the forest. Perhaps it is your house, Kian. A sapien is there – also a car, and maybe a crate. You should take these kittens, and go to see.'

'Oh no,' Kian started, 'I don't think that's my house –'

'How do you know?'

'Well, my –'

'You're not afraid, are you?'

Kian blinked at the sickly cat, who stared shrewdly back at him. 'No, I'm not afraid.'

'Well then.' The tom looked into the spanning branches. 'Janshar!'

There was no immediate response; then the ribbony gum leaves wavered and a voice asked sullenly, 'What?'

'Come here. I want to speak to you.'

Again there came a stubborn delay, and the black cat thinly yowled. A sinuous marmalade cat worked his way down the trunk of a manna gum then, crossing the damp earth languidly and slouching before the tom. 'What?'

The old cat peered at him. 'Janshar, you know where this house is?'

'. . . Yeah.'

'Then you must take these strangers to it – Kian fears going alone. You will enjoy the excursion: it's time you saw more of the world.'

Red Janshar looked across the creek, eyeing Kian uncivilly.

'All right,' he said. 'I can do that, if that's what you want, Givench . . . There's a dog at that house, you know.'

'So I've heard.' The tom narrowed crafty eyes. 'Do thoughts of a dog worry you, Janshar? Is that what you've grown to be, cowardly?'

Shyler snickered in the fern. 'He is, Givench. He's frightened of the hound.'

'Piss blood, Shyler,' snapped Janshar. 'No one asked you.'

'Crap thorns, fathead,' Shyler replied.

'There's no dog at my house!' Kian jumped to the bank, shouting over the bickery. He did not want to offend the black tom, let alone the entire clowder, by refusing their help, but the house they spoke of wasn't his, and he desperately did not want to waste time looking for it. 'This house can't be mine, because there are no dogs at my house!'

Givench's gaze skated to him. 'There's no dogs where you come from?'

'. . . Well, yes, there's dogs everywhere, they're a plague, but –'

'It could be the same house, then. Houses and dogs, both the same.'

'No, no, it's difficult to explain – my house is much further away, you see, there's no forest anywhere near –'

'They're afraid, Givench.' Shyler, lolling in the fishbone, sighed profoundly. 'It's one excuse after another. Scaredy-cats, the pair of them.'

The jibe flung Janshar into the fronds, spitting wrathfully. Shyler scuttled close to Tey, his ears flat on his skull. Givench watched placidly. 'Shyler,' he said, 'what a short life you will lead. Fleeting, but valiant. As you are so very brave, you must go too.'

'Me?' The grey tom gagged, swivelling stricken eyes to Tey. 'No! No, no, no!'

'Let him stay.' Janshar's tail was thrashing bitterly. 'He doesn't know his head from his arse.'

Tey had been studying Jem and Cally, who were hiding imperfectly behind Kian, and she took her attention to the spatting factions only reluctantly. She smacked a paw across Shyler's muzzle, the smoky cat being closer, and threatened Janshar with similar violence. 'Be quiet!' she snarled, and the younger cats cringed away. 'Both of you will go. Watch out for these cubs: if I hear you've done differently, crows will pick their teeth with you.'

She ducked into the scrub without a word or a glance behind her, leaving the toms glaring at each other and Kian watching despondently as the water clowder broke apart. The overcast faces seeped into the darkness and the trees were suddenly empty; the dappled female, Bodeyn, slipped along a crevice, Marlo ran downstream and disappeared. Black Givench stood on frail legs and shook himself vigorously, shedding a cloud of hair. To the five cats remaining by the water he said, 'Goodbye, then. Goodbye, little cubs.'

He crossed the supine tree-trunk and limped past the urban cats, a picture of pride and ruined majesty, his ears cut to pieces, his mask a network of scars. Kian, Jem and Cally watched him go and when they turned back to the feuding males they too had vanished, and the lost cats were alone.

Into the Forest

THEY SLEPT THAT night in the ferns around the creek, Kian catnapping between stretches of fidgety petulance. He watched Jem and Cally sleep the paralysed slumber of exhaustion and every atom in him urged him to leave, while they were peaceful and not looking. Night was sliding by him, its dark promise of secrecy squandered. But if the kittens weren't watching, others certainly were: Kian could feel a discreet observation of each flick of his ears and flex of his claws. These others would immediately recognise any spurning of their hospitality, and their graces, provoked, may not prove particularly good: a cat running away is a cat under attack. All this was not, however, the least of Kian's concerns. More than once his hair was ruffled by the inexplicable crying of the forest. It moaned and muttered to itself, groaning and whimpering; it sounded to the suburban cat as if every creature that ever died beneath the canopy was returned to melancholy existence with the rising of the moon. Kian was disturbed by the thought, and tried to stop thinking – sometimes, he knew, he thought too much. Finally, worn out with worry, faint with hunger, his mind spinning, his feet sore, trapped helplessly in the clutches of aggressively courteous, invisible cats, he propped his chin on his paws and went to sleep.

The morning sounds of the forest – birds greeting their neighbours with ringing calls across the sky, trees creaking as the sun warmed chilly branches, insects whirring their wings to get the flying-juices flowing – woke the refugees early; Kian opened his eyes and their pupils contracted fine as mantis legs, so glowy was the dawn. From deep within a lacy citadel of fern he sifted the air and detected, very thinly, the familiar fragrance of petrol. He bent an ear to the sound of the Earth and heard, with a sense of desolation, that his home had come no closer. He could smell ferals everywhere, but saw none of them.

Cally was wide awake and sitting up, fronds reflected in her amber eyes. 'We're still here,' she informed him.

'Yes.' He curled into a bundle, letting her huddle close to him. Morning had always been his favourite time of day, the pale immaculate summons to step from Ellen's bed or armchair and take up position by a kitchen cupboard, there to pace and wail discordantly in anticipation of breakfast. He could open the cupboard himself, if he put his mind to it, but the truth was he enjoyed the performing, the pacing and the wailing, and believed Ellen enjoyed it too. He had been in the middle of educating Jem and Cally in the art of pacing and wailing when events conspired to make the man come, and slung them into the box.

Kian did not think there had ever been a morning he disliked meeting as much as this one.

It was not until the sun had almost reached its zenith that Marlo emerged from the underbrush, walking on the stiff, experimental legs of the freshly-woken feline. The kittens, who had grown quickly bored with dismal Kian and the small twiggy arena in which he permitted them to play, were cautiously delighted to see the tabby and, after a moment's shy lingering under the fern, jumped about him joyfully. Sluggish with sleep, the young tom was taciturn. 'Come on,' he grunted. 'Tey says you have to eat.'

'Wait,' Kian said, and Jem and Cally stopped, looking back at him. He scoured the trees and rocks around which the water clowder had gathered but saw none of the ghostly faces that had haunted the scrub the night before. He knew they were there, though; the sense of being watched had not left him. He raised his voice so none could ever deny hearing it and said, 'Your troop has already been kind to us. It's not proper, now, for us to eat your food. The coldness is coming, and there's many of you to feed. What we three eat, you cannot. I'll take these kittens and hunt elsewhere.'

Marlo was inspecting a claw. 'Yeah,' he said, 'whatever.'

Kian, chary, searched the canopy: nothing moved or answered him, yet he was satisfied he'd been heard. He was also famished, and trotted across the creek after the younger cats. Marlo led them a short distance through the trees and halted on the brink of a pool of light, a radiance so unexpected in the dimness of the forest that Jem blinked and could not, for a moment, stop blinking. An immense eucalypt had toppled here, leaving a rupture in the canopy through which the muted autumn sunshine poured, lethargic as any cat. The light spilled over a rubble of pitted stone, and Kian, hunkering behind snakes of flayed bark, struggled to see what he was looking for. The stones appeared, to him, nothing more than stone – then something shifted, and his sights focused on the movement fast and sharp as a beam. Basking on the warm surface of the rock was a colony of glassy skinks, their eyes closed in stupor and their delicate limbs splayed. Kian stared, and sighed. He had, in his hunger, imagined a hunting ground packed with mighty reptiles, hearty meals in scales, but the biggest skink was the length of his longest whisker, and meagre as a fly. It would take him all afternoon to catch enough to even dent his appetite. His tail sagged with disappointment, but Jem and Cally stood braced with glee. 'Can we?' breathed the black kitten.

'Yes,' he said, 'go on.'

Into the sunshine they sprinted, the rocks bursting into flaring life as the lizards raced away. The tabby and the urban cat retired to the shade and watched the kittens leap and chase, scrabbling on the stone. 'Don't you like skink?' asked Marlo.

'I'm too lazy for skink.'

'Yeah,' the feral agreed knowingly, 'it's a cub's game. Maybe you'll get something to eat at the house.'

'I doubt it. It's not my house, you see.'

'Yeah, you said that before. No point going.'

Kian looked at the tabby. 'Then why must I go?'

'Who said you must?' The young cat flopped, luxuriating in ivy. 'No one said that. I heard Janshar and Shyler told to *take* you, and Givench will chew their tails if they don't do what they were told . . . but no cat ever said that you had to go.'

Kian swallowed a spitball of rage. 'But why – *why* must they take me *anywhere*? I am trying to get home!'

Marlo rolled over and stared at him, an ivy leaf stuck to his head. 'Don't you get it, cat? Shyler and Janshar have been chucked from the clowder. Making them take you to the house is Givench's way of getting them gone.'

There came a squeal from Cally, as Jem thefted a hard-won prize; Kian turned a distracted ear. 'They've been chucked from the clowder? What does that mean?'

'They've been *chucked*. Every tom born into the clowder gets chucked sooner or later. They get big, start to stink, quarrel with everyone, then they get chucked. The she-cats and the outside toms – toms like Givench, who live with the clowder but weren't born into it – they chase off the inborns before they make too much trouble. Janshar and Shyler looked like trouble, I guess.'

'Look at this, Kian!'

Jem had discovered that a skink's tail can wiggle with no skink attached, but what caught Kian's eye was the cloudy shadow he had seen before, the gauzy watcher of the forest darting flightily between the trees. It had no form, was no more than a moving smudge, yet it was clearly whole and alive. It paused when it saw him staring and although its translucent shape bore no face or expression Kian saw its curiosity and alertness and its restless, angry dismay. He asked the feral, 'What is that thing?'

'What is what thing?'

'. . . Don't you see it?'

The tabby sat up, specks of forest dropping from him. 'Don't I see what?'

The shadow swooped into the branches and swirled across the ground, silent, smooth as water. It flickered at the edge of the sunshine, shuddering with agitation. It sped around the eucalypts and Kian sensed its umbrage as Jem, oblivious, picked up and swallowed the remains of the lizard. To Marlo, who was puzzled, Kian murmured, 'Never mind.'

Marlo settled into the litter; Kian could not take his eyes from the tortured dance of the daemon and he was relieved when the shadow abruptly vanished, as if blown away by the breeze. He looked at Marlo, trying to remember what he'd been saying. 'What does a cat do,' he asked, 'after he leaves the clowder?'

'Get a territory, if he can. Or he might just wander around. He's not allowed back in the clowder, that's for sure, but why would he want to go back? All the clowder pussycats are related to him, so they won't give him any joy – oh, sorry.' The tabby cast a sideways glance at the urban cat. 'You're not-tom, aren't you? I forgot. You probably don't like hearing about pussycats. I can understand that.'

The favoured feline methods of capturing prey all involve waiting – waiting for a mouse to vacate its burrow, waiting for a bird to hop within pouncing range. The cat, therefore, is a creature of great patience, and Kian could call upon reserves of restraint to see him through the moment. Marlo, meanwhile, stood up and stretched his banded body, his tail curving over his head. He sat back down and said, 'What a cat does, after leaving the clowder, is make a life of his own. He's no cat's kitten any more. And I can't wait. You remember Whit and Loke? When I leave the clowder, I'm gonna be like them. Tough and nasty and no cat hassling me.'

'. . . I see. Why don't Janshar and Shyler want to leave?'

'Well, it's not that they don't *want* to. Every clowder-born male knows he'll have to leave – the outside toms remind him every day. I guess they're crabby because – well, what cat *likes* being told what to do? No cat. Do you think they *want* to take you to the house? No, they don't. That's why I'd keep my mouth shut, if I were you: they're gonna be spitting burrs bad enough already.'

'Yes,' the suburban cat muttered. 'I see.'

In the afternoon the kittens slept in the leaves, their bellies round and bulging; the skinks, drawn inexorably to the sun, were plucked one after another by Kian and Marlo, whose hunger had grown irresistible. Later the oily taste of them left Kian queasy and he lay in the litter watching the revived kittens romp with the feral. Cally charged through the underwood, hissing like a dragon; Jem gnawed her ear and she cheeped like a bird. The kittens sprang at each other and sprawled in dusty hammocks of ivy; they swarmed up and down tree-trunks and stalked one another's tails. Kian, his gut tightening against the slithery mass it contained, saw that, were they forced to stay in the forest, the kittens would go wild within days. They lacked loyalty, as do all young creatures: they were not missing the home he pined for, and they would never thank him for returning them there. But the urban cat did not let himself feel aggrieved – indeed, Kian was doglike in his inclination to make the best of things. He would submit quietly to being taken to the house, because that was the simple thing to do; once loosed of the tyrannical aid of the ferals, he would be free to speed home. Lying in the shadows with the fenny air of late afternoon thickening round him, the refugee tried to remember that whatever happens, happens for the best.

The red tom Janshar hit the ground behind him and Kian,

spitfiring, whirled from his reverie. The kittens fled into the bracken and growled at the feral from there. The tom was unimpressed by the tumult; to Kian he said gruffly, 'Ready?'

To cats, appearances are everything: a cat believes what he sees, rather than what he is told. Bluff and bravado are feline, and so too is beauty. With a single glance, every feature of the marmalade feral was etched into Kian's mind. Janshar was young, though fully grown; he was long and slim and carried himself close to the earth. His short coat was coloured a soft, creamy orange, and his face and body were unmarked by scars. He would have been a handsome cat, had not his bronze eyes been placed just slightly too close together: no cat would ever call another ugly, but Janshar's eyes lent him no dignity, for they made him look comical, and unfortunately kind.

'Janshar.' Marlo jumped from the lizard stones and stood boldly before the bigger cat, his tail confidently high. 'Let me come with you. I'm sick of living with the clowder, it's boring. I want to get out – I want to be a proper cat – come on, Janshar, let me.'

The red tom did not even swivel an ear; to Kian he said, 'This way.'

Kian mewed for the kittens and they skittered from the bracken, rushing to hide in his footsteps. Marlo stood alone as the cats walked away, his claws carving into the ground. He watched as they vanished in the massiveness of the forest, the landscape of fern and rangy heights of the trees. A black centipede was making its way across the stones and the tabby plucked it from the rubble, chewed it and spat it out. The ferns were waving in the strengthening breeze, the trees creaked with oncoming cold. Marlo told himself that, if the centipede still moved, he would follow the disappeared cats. If it, instead, showed no sign of life, he would return to the creek and await the nightly gathering of the water clowder. He held his breath and gazed at the arthropod. Mortally injured, it writhed on the stones. The tabby, pleased, trotted into the underbrush, keeping his cautious distance.

The Ochre Earth

THE FOUR CATS walking ahead of the tabby heard nothing of his progress. Janshar did not speak to or glance behind at the refugees clambering through the forest after him. Cally searched the blue-green scrub for Shyler but couldn't see the grey cat anywhere; the tom revealed himself eventually when the branch of a snow gum splintered and the kitten looked up to see the scraggy cat high above her head, threading his way through the canopy. Janshar did not lift his gaze to his brother feral, but a snarl crooked the corners of his mouth.

The cats proceeded into a scented dusk, leaving behind them the creek where the clowder assembled and the clearing where the fighting cats, Loke and Whit, had bailed up Kian. The trees thinned as they approached the road, the gravelled disfigurement cleaving the forest in two, and Shyler came down from the canopy. Kian stood on his toes and searched the weeds for the cardboard box, sensing it was near. A night and a day had passed since he'd arrived in the forest, yet he wasn't any closer to home – he'd returned, no less, to the place where he had begun. He fought down his frustration and followed the wild cats, who crossed the road confidently but without, he noticed, looking or listening for cars. On the far side of the road Janshar made a steep change of direction and Kian was jarred by the wrongness of this new bearing, deafened by the sudden disharmony of the Earth's guiding tune. He paused in the grass, his back arching, the breeze sheeting across the patchy ground. The kittens stopped beside him, nervous: 'What's the matter?' asked Cally.

The ferals had reached the cover of the fern and turned to stare at the halted refugees. 'What are you waiting for, cat?' called Shyler.

'He's afraid,' Janshar sneered.

Shyler ducked, to better see past the fern. 'You stand too long in the open,' he warned, 'and some owl will fly away with those kittens.'

'An owl?' Jem echoed. 'What's an owl?'

'You'll find out quick when one puts his hooks in you. Nothing fills an owly's gizzard quite as nice as a juicy kitten. Or maybe snake will come along and swallow you in a gulp.'

The eyes of the kittens blackened: 'A snake?' Cally whispered. 'Kian?'

'Go, then,' he said, and the young animals bolted, diving

headlong into the protection of the tangly scrub. Kian picked his way across the ochre ground to where the ferals sat waiting. 'Is that true?' he asked them. 'Would an owl take a kitten?'

'Why not?' Janshar stood and, with a shimmy of his tail, left his pungent mark dripping from the trunk of a tree-fern. 'Wouldn't you, if you were an owl?'

The twilight closed around the cats as they journeyed deeper into the forest, and with it rose a chorus of nocturnal noise. The urban cats flattened their ears to the scratching of mysterious creatures buried in the earth; they froze at the high-pitched piping of uncanny beasts and the approaching patter of urgent paws; their eyes flooded with the underworld screeching of something in the trees. Janshar snorted when he saw the lost cats cowering: 'What are you doing?' he snapped. 'Get up – you're embarrassing me!'

'What are you scared of?' Shyler pinned a slater and let it escape between his toes. 'Nothing in the forest is stronger or faster or cleverer than us – nothing has such cutting teeth and claws. The forest was made for cats to live in: you don't need to be afraid.'

But Kian was wary. 'What about the snake? What about the owl?'

Janshar sighed and resumed walking, twinging an intolerant tail. 'The owl takes the crippled cub, the sicky, the dolt. The snake takes the runt that's too small for the owl. It's good that kittens like that don't survive, to spread their faults and weaken us. The owl and the snake serve the cat – all the forest animals do. Most of them are only born to be feline thew and bone.'

'What do you mean, thew and bone?'

'Black halfwit, we eat them.'

'Oh.' Jem stepped carefully through a plantation of fungus, his paws powdered saffron with spores. 'You have to catch them first, though. You have to chase them and chase them and chase them.'

'So?'

Kian glanced behind at the kitten. 'Shush, Jem.'

'And all that just for lizards, and they don't even taste very good.'

'Jem, quiet now . . .'

'Be grateful you can do it, cub. That's a cat's life.'

'Not where we come from.'

'Jem! Quiet!'

The kitten blithely ignored Kian. 'Where we come from, the old woman chases our food for us, and puts it on a plate. Doesn't she, Cally? We don't have to hunt.'

Janshar's head jerked toward Kian. 'Is that true? You don't hunt?'

'Of course we do.' The black-and-white cat gazed into the distance as if something very interesting was happening out there. 'Often we do. Why wouldn't we hunt? We're cats.'

'Kian caught a mouse once,' Cally informed the ferals.

'He gave it to me though, because mice are just toys. That's what you said, remember, Kian? Mice are kitten toys.'

Janshar stopped; Shyler, too, looked back through loops of eucalypt bark, his tail waving slowly. 'A mouse is a meal to fill your stomach overnight,' stated the red tom. 'There's not much to him, but he's made of muscle and fat. What do you do, where you come from, if hunting is only a game?'

'We sleep,' Jem answered cheerfully, 'and eat. I don't think we do anything else. Do we, Kian?'

Kian didn't respond, slinking through the undergrowth as if unaware he was leaving the ferals and kittens behind. 'I wouldn't like to live your life, not-tom,' Janshar called after him. 'I wouldn't like to come from where you do. A cat has pride. A cat living your life might as well be a dog.'

Kian's ears folded and he growled in the throat. And I would not, he seethed, like to call this slippery, oozing, mouldery old forest my home. 'Let's get him,' he heard Janshar incite the kittens. 'Let's have him for a meal. Get down, be soundless, put your sniffer to the wind!'

Glancing back Kian was outraged to see Jem and Cally poised for pouncing, their eyes fixed brightly on him. 'Stop that!' he commanded. 'Stand up now!'

'They need to learn to hunt, cat –'

'No, they do not!' Kian snarled at the smirking ferals, his tail lashing to and fro. 'They don't live here, they don't need to learn about living here! Don't you go telling them anything: whatever they have to know, *I* will teach them.'

He turned and marched into the darkness, his riled blood thumping. He didn't know why he was so annoyed – he had, after all, little confidence in his ability to teach the kittens anything. Nevertheless his fury only escalated when he heard the ferals snigger and smelt the caustic odour of Janshar spraying another tree. 'You've got him worried now, cubs,' chortled the marmalade tom.

'He's too sour to eat,' said Shyler. 'Better just maul him.'

Kian lengthened his stride, pushing past low-slung leaves, his white whiskers tremoring as if blown by gusts of rage. Behind him, the excitement of the kittens buzzed like bees in the cold air. 'He's getting away!' yipped Janshar. 'Don't let him escape you! Go for his neck, cubs, separate his bones – go now, bring him down!'

Kian heard the kittens leap across the litter and suddenly he was running – he was flying. He flew, low to the ground, his hair slick to his frame. For a helter-skelter moment he raced mindless through the bracken, careless where he went, hoping only to be gone. Left easily behind, the kittens mewed with distress: the sound brought Kian to his senses and he discovered himself fleeing from cubs, his only possible motive being spleen and hurt vanity. He was galloping off in a sulk and the ferals were going to know it, and yowl mockingly. In this mortifying instant he saw, bunched in tangled shadows, a long-nosed, ratlike animal, its buff-coloured hindquarters slashed by sooty bands. It had no chance to look up from the specks it was eating before Kian was on it, had snatched it up and was tumbling, leaves flying everywhere, the unlucky creature gripped in four imprisoning paws. Shyler was instantly there, the storm-grey cat fast as fire and rumbling like thunder, grabbing for the prize – Kian spared a paw to drag four claws down the feral's angular face. The brittle skull of the marsupial popped with the force of his closing jaws and everything was bluntly finished; Kian allowed Cally to steal the carcass from him and she dragged it into the weedy gorse while her brother, bleating jealously, hovered in her wake.

The ferals were crouched amid honeysuckle, watching hungrily, intensely still. There were sticks in Kian's coat and dirt smeared on his chest as he stood before them, panting. 'I am a cat,' he said. 'You have your life, I have mine. But we are all cats.'

Janshar's eyes were black as kohl. 'Yeah,' he said, 'we're cats. And some of us can catch a bandicoot even by accident.'

Kian took the jibe without flinching. A cat sheds emotions as readily as hair and his anger, now, was gone; with the potent taste of blood in his mouth, his self-possession had returned. The ferals were only cats, callow and ill-fed ones at that: he did not need to fear them, or be bothered by their ridicule. He began to tidy his paws, saying, 'When the kittens finish eating, the three of us will walk back toward the road. That's the way we need to go. Thank you for your help, anyway.'

'. . . But you'll be going the wrong way. The house is up there, past that hill.'

'It's not my house, Shyler, and I don't need to see it. And I don't have to see it. Where I come from, cats do as they please, not as they are told.'

Janshar's stare hardened. 'We're only trying to help.'

'But you're not – you're not helping. None of this has helped. You've made me waste a day and half the night but I'm no closer to home – you've taken me further away.'

The wild cats glanced at each other. Kian continued to attend to his paws while the ferals exchanged harsh, muttered words. The half-moon was rising and the lost cat looked up to see the silhouette of five ducks crossing its lustreless face, each bird flying at an angle to its kin. In the scrub behind him Kian could hear Jem and Cally grizzling over the carcass, their tiny teeth grinding on cartilage, but there were no other sounds: whatever lived in this part of the forest was hiding, hoping the cats would go away. Over the mulch floated the watery scent of the area's owner and Kian hoped this cat would not return to refresh the markings while he himself was anywhere near. He had, he felt, encountered enough feral warlords for one lifetime. His keen eyes saw the canopy tremble and, suddenly nervous, Kian searched the branches for sight of the forest's shadow, sure the murder of a bandicoot would fill it with vengeful rage – then Shyler coughed, and he looked at the grey cat.

'Listen, Kian.' The smoky tom was casual, offhand. 'No cat tells *us* what to do, either. We do what we like. But Givench and Tey . . . well, they're old, and they're kind of crazy. They want you to see this house – it'll make them happy if you see the house. They'll feel like they've done something to help the kittens.'

'Givench and Tey aren't here,' answered Kian. 'So what does it matter, if we see the house or not? They will never know the difference.'

Janshar whined into the honeysuckle, his face crumpled with temper; Shyler considered the suburban cat before stepping out of the tendrils and stalking closer to Kian. 'Look, cat,' he confided, 'it's like this. There's eyes everywhere in this forest, and if we don't take you to the house like he told us to, Givench is going to hear about it. He holds grudges, Givench, he's full of old-cat spite. If we don't do like he said, Givench isn't going to be happy: from now on, any tom who wants to get in good with the clowder will try to impress him by taking a swipe at us. Imagine it – we'll be brawling from dawn to sundown, we'll never get a moment's peace! . . . All you need to do is look at it, Kian. You'd be doing us a favour.'

He felt the sore lack of favours done to himself, yet Kian was a fair-minded cat: after a lingering hesitation he said, 'It's close, this house?'

'We're almost there. You never know, we might pick up a meal. Where there's sapiens, there's always rats.'

Kian glanced at Janshar, who kept the stony reticence of one who wishes he were elsewhere. The red tom was younger and lighter than Kian, but the suburban cat saw no wisdom in provoking the feral's irritability. He could not risk injury to himself, when he had so much further to travel: even the most arrogant cat understands that, sometimes, the smart thing to do is comply. 'All right,' he sighed. 'I'll look at it. Then I must get home. We'll wait, first, for the cubs.'

Janshar groaned, slumping into the creeper; Kian walked away and sat down alone. The older cats were silent as the kittens, hidden in the gorse, noisily devoured the marsupial. The grainy dusk had given way to a smooth, ink-dark night, a swathe of navy silk draped across the sky. Kian groomed his rumpled coat and lent only one ear to Shyler, who lazed on his back studying the refugee through mild, grass-green eyes. Eventually the feral asked, 'Why are you in such a hurry to leave, cat? Don't you like the forest?'

Kian muzzled into himself, tugging at the tangles. He could feel a distinct scurrying as he worked – the company of the wild cats was coming complete with fleas. 'I like the forest,' he replied, 'but it isn't my home.'

'Tigers live in forests,' said Janshar. 'Forests are good enough for tigers, but not good enough for you.'

'I am not a tiger.' Kian shook his coat into order. 'I am a cat. I have a territory, and I've lived on it all my life. Everything is mine there, everything smells of me. I belong there, so I have to leave here. Your forest is beautiful, but it isn't mine.'

Janshar's tail swatted the leaves. 'What about the sapien? You're her feline mutt, aren't you? You're going home to her.'

Kian glanced into the gorse, making certain the kittens were absorbed in eating and unlikely to overhear. Jem was chewing lethargically on the bandicoot's stringy tail; Cally, her face bloody, lay over the corpse in a stupor. Kian looked back at the ferals. 'There's spiders in my territory,' he said, 'and many birds. There's insects of every shape and kind. There was an ancient woman, too, but she was no more important to me than the bugs or spiders or birds. I'm not going home to a sapien: I'm going home to my land, to the grass and concrete, to the place that owns me. You would understand, maybe, if you had territories of your own.'

'I'll get a territory,' Janshar said smartly. 'Don't think I won't get one.'

Shyler blinked at the stars. 'Not me,' he sighed, 'I don't want a range. All that defending and patrolling, makes a cat feel tired. I'm going to be a wanderer, free as a gale, a whip-poor-will. You'll never know where I am – one moment I'll be here, the next moment, gone!'

Bohemian talk offended Janshar, who smacked the lazing feral across the mouth; Shyler sprang to his feet and launched at his attacker, who was already swinging viciously as the grey tom came at him. Kian, unmoved, sat in the blackness, a scuffed-up shower of dirt and leaves raining on his cleaned coat. Shyler screeched and scurried into the darkness, shaking his battered head. Honour mangled, he spluttered, 'You pusbag – you doghole! The only way *you'll* get a territory, Janshar, is by snatching it from some puny malkin – some half-dead she-cat! Any other feline will pull you from your skin!'

'Come here and say that, scrote!'

The sound of the scuffle had roused Jem and Cally, who crawled from the gorse and pondered the ferals numbly. Jem yawned. 'Are we going?'

'We are,' said Kian, and led the kittens away before the wild cats could exhibit any more of their vulgar habits. In his mind, Shyler's accusation – that Janshar would only get a territory by stealing the land from a weaker cat – was settling gently as dust. The ferals abandoned their spat and loped after the refugees, leaping the place where the bandicoot had been grazing and where a hank of Kian's snowy belly hair, snagged on the point of a stick, blew light as dandelion seed, shining beneath the moon.

High up on a branch of the canopy Marlo stretched his legs, ripping off chips of bark. He had been a fascinated spectator to the various happenings on the forest floor, having scaled the tree while the journeying cats were distracted by the marsupial kill. The smell of the slain bandicoot had made the tabby's stomach gurgle, loudly enough, he'd feared, to betray his presence and wreck his game; fortunately the attention of the cubs was with the carcass, and the bigger cats, typically, were thinking of themselves. He had watched and listened from his vantage-point, gripping the branch as it shifted with the breeze. The conversation he heard had not interested him, but the fact that he could hear it filled him with a smug sense of mastery. Now, the cats gone, he slid down the gum's brindled trunk and groomed himself quickly before speeding on toward the house, choosing a route that would hide him from the travelling cats until the perfect moment came.

The Shivering Bracken

THE FIVE CATS stood on the crest of the hill, staring down at the house. Behind them the land cleaved into a gully and exuded a rimy arctic air as if from frostbitten lungs. The gully sheltered a vein of rainforest where massive blackwoods and magnificent sassafras grew, and the boughs of a lonely shining gum seemed to grapple with the moon. Ahead of the cats stretched a slope of grassy land saturated by evening dew and nestled at the base of the slope was a small farmhouse with its chimney uncoiling a thread of dry-leaf smoke. The cats stood on a verge of rock which severed the rainforest from the open land as cleanly as lightning splits a tree. Jem sniffed, his black nose creasing. To Kian he murmured, 'Something smells yuck.'

'That's sapien stink,' said Shyler.

'Ellen doesn't smell like that.'

'It is human stink, though,' agreed Kian.

'There's something else, too,' said Janshar.

'Cows?' Shyler suggested. 'They're whiffy.'

'No.' Janshar's whiskers shivered. 'Something else. Bird. Blood.'

'Dog, too,' said Kian.

The cats gazed into the valley, lacking the energy to decide what to do. A cat can stalk a sparrow by tracking the odour of its spindly footsteps, and Kian, high on the ridge, could detect in the swirling wind traces of gas and metal, petrol, gravel, porcelain and plastic, scents which he knew from his own home and which made his heart beat anxiously. He saw a car, a coop, a fence; there was muffled light glowing beyond a curtained window and clothes hanging lank on a line. He saw a pair of leather boots toppled beside the door. This was not his house and something about it made him apprehensive but still he wished he had been wrong, that the house tucked into the valley had been his house, after all.

'Well,' said Janshar, 'that's that.'

Kian chirruped to the kittens, who weaved after him as he slouched back into the forest; the wild cats turned and followed. The gully wall was steep and the cats picked a path down it, placing each paw cautiously before shifting weight onto it. Layers of ferns built tall barricades, the plants so crammed and solid they appeared easier to climb over than push through; the cats were scratched squirming past them, and showered with dew. The floor of the rainforest was cushioned with moss that spangled in the moonlight and preserved the indentations of their tentative feet. A wad of leaves loosened under Cally and slid away with the calico kitten wide-eyed upon it; Jem bounced after her, grabbing at the leaves, and when the wad broke apart with his mangling his sister was sent sprawling. Kian and the ferals, daubed with soil and dew, found their way to a tablet of rock which rose from the moss and lay flat enough to let them sit down and rest. They brushed their ears and licked their flanks and shook each leg vehemently so not a fleck could cling. When he was trim and sleek once more Kian reached down, touching a paw to the earth. He felt its guiding thrum reverberate along his bones. 'I have to go this way,' he said, pricking his ears to the breeze.

'. . . We'll walk with you a bit.'

'Thank you, but you needn't. You have better things to do, I'm sure.'

More often than not cats conclude even the most fleeting of their dealings with one another on an antisocial note – it is almost a point of feline honour, to close an encounter with either or both of the parties wishing they had never met. Kian resented the ferals for wantonly wasting his precious time; the ferals, for their part, begrudged him for intruding on theirs. With cool courteousness, ears up and tail down as if blissfully unaware of the stickiness of the situation, Kian stepped from the rock and, in two bounds, leapt to where Jem and Cally lay. The urban cats would have walked off and soon vanished had not a distant sound caught Kian's attention, and made him freeze. It was not a loud noise, but it was choppy and crowded, many things tripping over each other within its tumultuous confines. Inside the noise rolled clods of dirt, branches broke and swags of leaves were ripped in tatters from trees; to Kian it sounded as if small chunks of forest were being gouged up and hurled aside. The kittens cringed, confused, and Kian looked around to see the ferals, tautly alert, staring toward the rocky verge. 'What is it?' he asked, though he had a sinking feeling he already knew.

The wild cats didn't answer. They scrutinised the rain-forest, scanning the lichened trunks of gigantic blackwood and beech, skimmed the mildewed ground. They sniffed the air and their hackles spiked, prickling their tails. From behind the walls of fern came a shouted bellow and the verdant barricade shuddered; Shyler, on his haunches like a rabbit, was the first to see what was coming and gasped, '*Run!*'

The five cats bolted, each flying instinctively from the others as if solitude alone could save it. Cally raced across the pulpy earth and plunged in a thicket of blackberry and clematis, burrowing blindly into its thorny maw. The noise, having crashed its way down the gully, boomed all around her now, resounding off the rainforest's ceiling. The little kitten squirmed until she could bury herself no deeper; then, her claws hooked to the blackberry's canes, she turned to face bravely the thing she knew she would see.

In her short life Cally had come nose to nose with very few dogs but, in common with all domestic felines, she had been born with a detestation for the enemy sunk into her core: a kitten will spit at the stench of canine even before her eyes unseal and she can see her boisterous foe. The dog scuffling at the blackberry thicket was the biggest animal Cally had ever seen; its huge ears flapped atop a stocky head and its jaws came together with a sound like rocks colliding. It forced its snout into the blackberry, shaking off the tendrils that scratched at its eyes; its strong legs scored the crumbly earth, throwing up plumes of dirt. It rammed its head forward and Cally saw her stricken face reflected in flashing eyes; it barked deafeningly, lassoing her with a rope of slaver. She held to the canes with all her strength as the blackberry was trampled and torn; her tiny mouth opened and she hissed, ready to lash for the beast's nose when it was shoved within striking range. The dog's jaws were open and the frowsty fume of meals past swelled out with each heave of its lungs; its teeth were long scimitars and Cally glimpsed the tongue flopping between them, pink and soaking. She loosened her grip as the nose pushed nearer and hissed again, loudly, but less enraged, and more afraid. The dog whined and pranced backward and Cally suddenly realised that it was not looking at her – if it had seen her, it was ignoring her. She looked up and saw, perched haphazardly in the knots above, the young striped tabby Marlo. He was clinging to a cane that bent malevolently with his weight and when he saw her staring he unlocked his teeth to splutter, 'Isn't this fun?'

The words electrified the dog, which wailed piercingly and surged into the thicket: Cally and Marlo, desperate and unable to retreat further, swung their armoured paws. Neither punch connected: the blackberry absorbed the dog's propulsion and flung it back powerfully at the beast, who lost its balance and fell hard in the leaves but was up again in an instant, its sights on something new. A short gawky sapling was growing on the fringe of the blackberry and the dog rushed at it, baying hysterically. Cally, peeping through the leaves, saw Shyler and Janshar stranded on the sapling's highest branch, struggling to hold to the tottering tree; the dog, however, was hurling itself at a black-and-white bundle that clung pathetically to a flimsy twig, perilously low to the ground. Kian flinched as the great jaws scissored upward, his whiskers blown askew as the staked scarlet cavern smashed closed. He dared not climb higher, nor spring for any nearby tree; his place on the branch so insecure, he could not even brandish a paw. The dog understood the cat's predicament and leapt at the tree, deranged with joy, paws scrabbling, fur flying, its face sudsy with spittle. The sapling lurched as the animal slammed its trunk, the threadbare canopy threshing. The forest shook with the dog's uproar; flocks of birds burst crying into the night and the massive rainforest trees shed a protest of bark and leaves. The dog jumped and stumbled, kicking up soil and litter; it jumped and fell and was unexpectedly quietened by the pain of its own bitten tongue. Janshar, his paws grouped dainty as petals and his ears held confidently upright, filled the ringing silence by asking, 'Is this the best you can do, cur?'

The dog, used to smart-mouthed felines, ignored the feral. It trotted briskly back and forth before the sapling while it caught its breath, its sienna eyes fixed on Kian. The scuffed square ears slapped against its long head; its coat, brown as topaz, was studded with grass seeds. 'Kitty kitty kitty,' it panted, exhaling the word on each tread of a foot. 'Kitty kitty kitty kitty . . .'

'Mongrel knave,' said Shyler, staring imperiously from the branch. 'Where are your brothers, pack-beggar? Why are you alone? Does the pack hate you? Has it cast you out, lump-licker?'

This was a familiar and reliable taunt between the species: centuries of twined, antagonistic history had taught each party the quickest means of affronting the other and the language in which to do it, although canines lack the feline's abusive skill. The dog, retaliating, lifted its leg against the sapling, and the ferals snarled at the rising vapour. 'Worm-bags!' it wolfed. 'Vermin! Vermin on a stick.'

'Better run for your human.' Janshar's tail whisked lividly. 'Ask him what to do. Can't do anything without sapien's say-so, can you, slave? You're a disgrace to your ancestors – no lupus would recognise you, groveller, whimperer, scratcher-at-the-door.'

'Pinheads!' The dog roared at Janshar but it was Kian it went for, gape-jawed; the suburban cat hugged the jouncing branch, desperately hissing. The dog ricocheted off the tree and hit the ground heavily, baying dementedly. 'Pestilence!' it shouted. 'Lickspitters! Ringworms, hookworms, tapeworms!'

'Arse-snuffler knows his parasites,' observed Shyler.

'Shit comes out both ends of puppy-dog,' said Janshar.

The hound lifted its snout and wailed. 'Blight feral! Shoot feral! Poison feral! Cage feral, skin him rabbit-nude! Feel the cold then, kitty kitty!'

'Shut your meathole, mound-maker,' Shyler said, but distractedly – Cally saw the tom was searching for a route of escape. Janshar, too, was sifting the surrounds, keeping the dog only on the edge of his vision. When the dog leapt again at the tree, the red cat lashed out with sudden impatience, slitting the beast's nostril in two. The sting of the laceration sent the animal insane: forgetting Kian, it lunged for the ferals, flinging its muscled body skyward. If it expected the pair to scatter, however, its calculations were direly wrong. Instead of fleeing, the cats attacked. They let the beast bring its head to them, and then they wrapped themselves around it.

The cry that came from its throat was terrible, the shriek of a grown dog reduced to a helpless puppyhood. Blindfolded by Janshar it landed oafishly and reeled onto its back, its tail pulled ruefully between its legs, the legs themselves kicking the air. The ferals swarmed over the animal's face, their hind claws stripping hair, their teeth stabbing through tough skin. The tabby Marlo was irresistibly drawn: he shot from the bracken to the enemy's chest and for a moment it seemed the unfortunate dog had been doused by a cauldron of curses which had somehow taken the form of cats, so agonised were its howlings, so tortured were its writhings, so mercilessly did the assailants shred their victim. The dog wrestled loose but made no attempt to salvage its mutilated pride: tail tucked pitifully, spine bent with fear, the scorch of poisoned claw-wounds spurring it along, it tore off through the rainforest yelping shamelessly as it went. The cats cantered after it a short distance before stopping to watch it go. 'Cretin,' Shyler muttered.

Both toms looked, then, at Marlo, who quailed and toadied but failed to mollify Janshar, who beat him on the head. The young cat protested, 'If you'd let me come with you, this would never have happened!'

They did not need to hear the details of how he came to be where he stood – they could smell his story in his coat and whiskers and impressed on the pads of his paws. After leaving the place where Kian had killed the bandicoot the striped feral had hurried to reach the farmhouse, meaning to surprise the travellers when they arrived. While the five cats stood on the ridge staring down at the house, Marlo had been underneath it, staring up at them. He had been waiting there for some time already and was rather cramped and cold; the reek of dog had gone to his head, leaving him edgy and excited. When he saw the cats retreat into the rainforest he'd stayed where he was, puzzling what to do. His plan evidently gone awry, he felt a little foolish. He was not sure, now, that the plan itself had ever been anything other than hare-brained. In common with many young animals, young cats are indecisive, and Marlo could not decide whether to follow the travellers into the rainforest or to slink back to his creekside home. While he'd deliberated he had toyed with a chicken feather, which smelt strongly of blood; the feather stuck to his nose and then to his tongue and it was simplest, in the end, to eat it. Above him he heard the dog's tail smack the floorboards and the rumbling sounds of the man, and Marlo was suddenly certain of one thing: with a sapien and a canine over his ears, this was no place for a lonesome feline. He wanted the security of the forest, where he could think from the height of a tree. He had wriggled out from beneath the house and it was an unfortunate coincidence that the man put the dog out at exactly the same time.

'I didn't mean to lead it to you,' he swore to the ferals, and felt no compunction doing so – a half-truth is, to a cat, quite as good as a whole. In reality he had sprinted like a possessed thing to the verge where the travellers had stopped, and as he'd led his slathering pursuer into the rainforest he'd been searching frantically for any sign of the five cats. If he could find them, his chances of losing the dog would improve vastly; if not, he was prepared to meet his destiny. True to his feline nature, he did not for a moment wonder if the travellers were prepared to meet theirs. Now he added greasily, 'But I knew you two could carve him.'

The toms deserved the flattery – before the midnight encounter, neither of them had ever been so close to a dog – but no cat accepts a compliment gracefully. The ferals puffed themselves up and strutted, sidetracked utterly from their annoyance, and arrived back at the blackberry in the most amicable of humours. Kian blinked at them from the sapling, and Cally gazed between the canes. Jem, who had hidden throughout the fracas in a creeping of ivy and who had several times been trodden on by the rampaging dog, pricked his ears at the sight of Marlo. But none of the urban cats moved to forsake their shelter and Shyler asked finally, 'Are you waiting for cur to chase you out?'

Kian slipped head-first down the tree, and the kittens, reassured, scrambled into the moonlight after him.

Misty Morning

KIAN WAS BEDRAGGLED, his coat matted, his claws ragged, his face flecked with dog slobber. One of his ears was nicked – he had no idea how that happened – and the blood had hardened crustily. He was a finicky cat and couldn't abide a slovenly hair but he did not ask the ferals if they might wait while he straightened himself. Shyler and Janshar were as filthy as he, but they did not seem perturbed. In the wild, Kian supposed, there were more important things to worry about than good grooming.

Shyler's question was not entirely a joke: it was possible that the dog might return, dangerous with plots of revenge. No wild cat could live happily in the rainforest, so near to the house of the canine, but Janshar made a quick circuit of the area spraying news of his victory on stones and trees, hopeful some feral might happen by. Then he turned to Kian, asking, 'Well, which way? Where's this territory you're always moaning about?'

Kian glanced apprehensively at the tom. 'It's a long way from here, Janshar. It might not be where you want to go.'

'There's territory all over: every direction's the same to me. Yours is as good as any other. What about you, Shyler?'

The slate tom tweaked his coat. 'I'm a rambling cat,' he said. 'I'm a leaf on the breeze.'

Kian stared at them, astonished: he realised that, not only were the ferals promising never to lead him further astray, but they were offering, against the unknowable forest, the gift of their courage and experience. His nerves racked by the dog attack, by the murk of the forest, by fear and disorientation, by the oppressive shadowing of the forest's dark heart, he was so grateful to them that he sprang larkishly into the air and, landing, bounced sideways on his toes. The wild cats reacted instantly: the big ferals rushed at him, baring fangs, while Marlo simply vanished. Kian cowered, seeing his mistake, and Janshar, hopelessly confused, screamed, 'Cat, what are you *doing*?'

'I was just . . . playing . . .'

'*Playing*? You're not a kitten!'

'I'm sorry.' Kian mumbled into the dirt. 'I didn't mean to . . . Don't you . . . play?'

'We stop playing when we leave the teat – playing is for cubs! Why would a grown cat play? What a waste of energy!'

Shyler's lip curved; he said, 'You're strange sometimes, cat.'

Kian gazed at his grubby paws, wishing the earth would swallow him. Ferals, he told himself, are gladiators: they do not trouble over appearances, and they do not play. The gaffes he could make, in the eyes of these cats, were nearly limitless – it was horrible just thinking of it. He wondered if there was anything about him that they might find awe-inspiring, and humbly understood there was not. Haggard and traumatised, Kian felt himself to be a particularly unimpressive cat. The crowning achievement of his career as a ferocious predator had been his raid on the myna's nest: both adult birds had gone for him, their butter-yellow beaks aimed at his eyes, but he had singlemindedly braved the rancorous defence and at one stage even batted the male of the pair from the sky. He had been immodestly proud of the deed ever since but, witnessing the ferals' pummelling of the dog, Kian recognised he had never achieved a thing. In his life he had encountered canines innumerable, he'd seen dogs made in every colour and size, he'd run from most of them and stood his ground to a few, but he had never gone for a hound as the wild cats had, so boldly, almost eagerly. Had he been left to save himself Kian would, he knew, still be up the sapling. He felt warmed with pleasure to remember that the dog had mistaken him for a feral, had even addressed him by that word, *feral,* but he also knew that the wild cats were demeaned by the faulty association. He drew a heavy breath; the ferals still glared at him crossly and he said, 'You were very brave, back there. You were heroic.'

Marlo, stealing out of the scrub, said, 'That? That was nothing.'

Shyler asked, 'Which way, cat?'

Kian turned his ears to the call in the ground. 'This way.'

So the six felines left the shattered blackberry and strolled into the night, Marlo skulking along in wise silence, the kittens romping ahead but glancing behind always to check the older cats were there. They clawed their way up the steep gully wall as the forest, recovering from the dog's invasion, came back to busy life: interred crickets began to sing, gliders spruced their flying capes, owls shook their weighty wings. Kian felt his blood hum with the satisfaction it was, to finally orient himself to the correct stars and tune; as he crossed the sea of native violet which separated the rainforest from the shambling stands of mountain ash, messmate, acacia and tree-fern, in his mind Kian was roaming the metallic and plastic surfaces of his distant suburban home. This was the second night he'd been absent from his range and he wondered what had already gone amiss. His speckled neighbour would certainly be sniffing around the inexplicably vacated territory, ready and willing to annex the land. The faintness of the Earth's call told Kian his journey would fill many nights and days; once home, it would be the occupation of a season to reclaim the sovereignty he would lose during this absence, a season of the most vigilant scratching and shrieking and bawling. Maintaining a territory was a fulfilling but unabating chore – he wondered if Janshar, intent on establishing a range of his own, knew quite what it was he was wishing. The red cat was sauntering alongside Kian and the urban cat eyed the feral tom. Janshar was fast approaching his prime; slender and athletic, his whimsical wide-eyed expression did not disguise the aggressive self-assurance behind each footstep. He was leaving his mark on tree stumps and broken limbs, proclaiming to the local cats that a feral such as he had passed by – the smell of it was making Kian nauseous. But Janshar had lived his life under the protection of the creek clowder and Kian doubted that the tom had ever been embroiled in genuine combat or had yet learned real fighting skill: he recalled Shyler catcalling that Janshar's best hope of securing a territory lay in poaching one from a weaker animal. The pupils of Kian's lime eyes dilated and constricted and dilated again. He knew that Janshar viewed him as an inferior, and it occurred to him that the tom had asked a lot of questions about Kian's territory while they'd waited, earlier that night, for the kittens to eat the bandicoot. True, the marmalade cat scorned the notion of metropolitan life . . . but perhaps his attitude was a clever ruse, and perhaps he was sniggering as he let Kian, the naive sap, lead him voluntarily home to an unpromised land. It would be, after all, much easier for Janshar to wrest territory from a cat like Kian than to challenge a beast like the warrior Loke. Kian's heart clenched with foreboding; he coughed, and the wild cats looked at him. 'You would hate living where I live,' he said stumblingly. 'You would think it very dull. Nothing exciting happens – not like here, in your forest.'

'Are you still thinking about that dog?' Shyler creased his iron-grey nose. 'Your life *must* be boring, if you reckon *that* was exciting.'

Jem, who was boxing a mushroom across the mulch, remarked with some relish, 'That dog wanted to eat Kian.'

'Yeah, it did.' Janshar wagged his tail jauntily. 'Did you see how it went straight for you? Serves you right for being shiny.'

Kian used his whiskers to probe, in the darkness, the distance between two close-growing trees: the arching ivory-white sensors judged the space wide enough to accommodate his body, which followed them confidently through. 'That brawler Loke said something about me being shiny. What does it mean?'

Marlo seemed enchanted by the question: he sprinted up a messmate and dived head-first into the ground. 'Don't you get it? Look at you – you look like you've been running in snow!'

Kian glanced over a shoulder and along the length of his spine. His head, ears, flanks and tail were all glossy black, but his legs, belly and throat were white, as were his chin and the flag-end of his tail. The hair inside his ears was white, he knew, as were his whiskers and the blaze down his nose. He had always been proud of his lean and lanky looks – he was elegant, oriental. 'So?' he asked huffily.

Marlo spun a circle, thrilled. 'Cat, how can you disappear when you're glowing like a star? There's nothing white in the forest – nothing but you! Everyone sees you, even if they don't want to!'

And the tabby galloped through the scrub, unhinged by delight. Kian looked at Janshar and Shyler and with nonchalant malice the red tom confirmed, 'He's right, you know. White's the worst way to be. It's an unlucky kitten who's born shiny here – that's a cat who never lives long. White's a misfortune that makes life hard. Hard to sneak up on a keen-eyed bird, hard to hide from the cur.'

Kian stared at his companions, shadow-cats in moonlight. The nocturnal hues of Jem and Shyler absorbed them in the darkness; the mottled shades of Janshar and Cally camouflaged them in the sun. Marlo, clad as he was in the primeval colours, was an invisible cat anywhere. Kian shook a paw reflexively, as if to flick off whiteness like water. Cally came to him, touching her brow to his chin: in response he hissed at her banefully, and sprang up the rump of a nearby rock. He could feel the forest watching him, motionless as a cat stalking a thrush. 'This way,' he said brusquely. 'We have to go this way.'

They continued their journey on through the blackness, sometimes veering far from each other, sometimes drawing close. Silence fell ahead of them, chatter and squeaks resumed in their wake. The ferals stopped to investigate every claw-gouge on the trees and to flehm the coasting, moist night air. In the darkest pit of the night they heard the unearthly growl of an irate cat and, looking up, were awed to see a hulking battle-scarred warrior snarling down from the canopy, frizzed with rage at this intrusion into its territory: 'Leave!' it gargled, 'Leave!' and they did, skittering away with their ears flat as leaves.

As dawn approached they travelled like clouds, soft and soundless on muffled feet, sweeping the understorey for hint of any animal returning, slow and full-bellied, to its daylight hideaway. Shyler put his nose to the soil and tracked a mouse which had signposted its route with the scent of itself but it was Jem who discovered the little rodent and cuddled his prize to him, racing with it to the tip of a peppermint's branch, where the ferals could not follow. Woozy moths made easy pickings for the other cats, but Kian, who had eaten almost nothing for two days and who, unlike the intrepid kittens, viewed with despair the prospect of securing his meals through skill and ambition, found and defended and revived himself on the rigid corpse of a bat which had died of old age at some point in the night. He ate every scrap of it, even the bony feet and flavourless ears. Sated, the cats dissolved into the scrub and slept until the sun was high.

Jem, draped along the peppermint's branch, woke to the

sound of voices; peering down sleepily he saw Kian sitting with Shyler and Janshar, the suburban cat tending his coat while the ferals lazed on their sides. Marlo was crouched beneath a tree-fern, chewing on a stick; in the shade behind the feral, Cally's eyes glinted like garnets, scrutinising each twitch of the tabby's banded tail. Jem yawned, his pink tongue curling, and stretched his legs to the points of his claws. He hung his head over the limb and rotated an ear to listen, his eyes closing drowsily.

'You worry too much,' Shyler was saying. 'What do you care what a dog says? Don't give him the satisfaction. Dogs are mongrels, they're toads.'

'You don't need to tell *me* about dogs,' retorted Kian. 'Where I come from, there are more dogs than pussycats. Every day I cross the path of some stinking hound or another: I know dogs very well.'

'More dogs than pussycats?' The ferals glanced at each other, and Kian's tail switched testily.

'That cur meant what it said – it hadn't dreamed those things. If there's traps and poison in the forest, you should tell me.'

'And I suppose *your* home is perfect.'

'Well, there's no . . .' Kian paused, his sights caught on the red cat. It occurred to him that he was not obliged to tell Janshar anything good about his home. 'No,' he said, 'my home's not perfect. Far from it, Janshar.'

'Exactly.' The marmalade tom tucked his paws against his chest. 'There's no place that's perfect for a cat – not any more. The forest's got trees for climbing and soil for scratching and stones for leaving a mark: there's sun and wind and shelter and shade, and there's no creature so gifted in the crush and lacerate – but the forest's no more perfect than any other place cats have been since the night we walked off the savannah into the monkeyman's firelight. We've spread and multiplied since that night, there's nowhere unstamped by the prints of our paws . . . but we sailed from savannah on an ocean of blood. The sapien's always treated a cat's life as the cheapest of things. We should have left him to the mercy of his vermin.'

Kian and Shyler said nothing: every cat born knew well the sad chronicle of feline past. It was a tale without conclusion, as carefully groomed as Kian's flyaway coat. It had neither variation nor moderation in its telling, for cats cling steadfastly to their chosen version of the facts. It was a legend drenched in gore told by every queen to her cubs, a story Jem had remembered when Ellen held him for the first time. Miaowing piteously to be freed, his tiny claws had snagged in her clothes and he'd looked as if he could not, on the contrary, bear to let her go. It was a tale that, given the slightest opportunity, no cat could resist telling, for the drama of martyrdom is quite appealing to felines.

'Ancient Bubastis was the Nile territory of Bast, the sapien goddess with the cat's head. The Nile sapiens claimed to worship and adore us, red Ra was a tom cat, their god-thing of the sun . . . but no true cat was ever warm on a stone Bubastis hearth. Instead our necks were broken and our bodies tied in rag so the corpses could be sold like trinkets and buried in the sand, offerings to that feline-faced slut Bast. Comets passed and the time came when a pitch cat was a cat who wouldn't breathe long, an unfortunate time to be born any cat or colour at all.'

The haw was seeping torpidly over Shyler's grass-green eyes. 'They drowned cats, the scrotes. Forced them into sacks and sank them in the water. Forced them into more sacks and set the dogs on them. Locked them up in baskets and hung the baskets over flames. They threw cats from clifftops to see us smashed to pieces, they pushed us into cages and then stabbed us through. They were trying to get the witch out, whatever witch is.'

'Yeah, witch is a mystery. Maybe it's our speed, or our cleverness. Maybe it's the fact we don't grovel like the hound. What do you think, cat?'

'I don't know.' Kian was fiddling with a nut-brown seed-pod and did not look up. 'I don't care, either. My mother said that witch isn't something inside cats, but something that lives in sapiens. She said they were trying to put in us a thing they didn't want in themselves.'

Janshar, who was not philosophical, was regretting he had asked. 'Well,' he said, 'whatever it is, they can't have thrashed it out of every cat, or there'd be none of us anywhere. Instead we're here, there and everywhere, we've chased the mouse around the globe – but we're always badgered, wherever we are. Look at you, Kian, and those harmless cubs. You've been chucked from a place you thought was your own. Why? What did you do?'

'It *is* my own,' Kian said quickly, 'and I've done nothing wrong.'

'Maybe you haven't – but you *are* a cat. The chronicle proves it: persecution prowls in the footsteps of the cat. Look at us: we were born in this forest, and this is our home. So why do we have to run from dogs? Why do we have to beware steel cobwebs? Why do we sniff poison in every tempting chunk of meat? We had no choice in being born, and now we are simply trying to stay alive: why, then, are we always afflicted, why so encouraged to die?'

'Maybe it's Bast we offend.' Shyler spoke from behind closed eyes. 'Maybe she wants our heads, to add to her collection.'

'Bast!' Janshar snorted. 'Squirt on that bitch. Cats have survived everything, but where's the goddess now? She's faded away like smoke. Her worshippers forgot her and she starved for lack of admiration. A goddess is nothing but a puff of wind, a god is a dustmote given a name – a *wish*, that's all they are. Every creature is made of flesh and blood – what use to us are phantoms who never go hungry or hurt from a wound? They're nothing but cowardice masquerading as courage: any dignified animal would be embarrassed to conjure such trolls.'

Janshar set his jaw; his abrupt silence made the cats aware of the daytime around them, the sheer clean air smelling raw with coming rain, the whistle and chime of robins, honey-eaters and rosellas, the piping of a kestrel hovering beyond the canopy. The burnished shell of a cockroach cracked as Marlo broke it into pieces. Kian tapped the seedpod and it twirled into the wreckage of a parched, skeletal fern. He said, 'I've run from dogs before – there's not a cat breathing who hasn't. But I don't know what steel cobwebs are, and what's poison doing inside meat?'

Janshar quavered his pale whiskers. 'A steely cobweb can't snare a butterfly, but it can catch a cat. If it captures you, you won't be seen again, so be careful where you tread. The poison waits to bleed your life out through your nose: be certain what you're eating smells only like itself, and never eat anything that seems too good to be true.'

'Well,' said the urban cat, 'I'm pleased to say I haven't.'

'It's not a joke, Kian. Countless cats lost their heartbeats so you could be given this advice.'

The refugee ducked his head apologetically; he watched the haw slide from Shyler's eyes as the feral stood and flexed in ritual order his shoulders, spine, legs and toes, specks of damp leaf litter raining from his coat. Janshar got up and shook himself, orange hair hazing the air. 'Come on,' the tom said. 'We're wasting dry weather.'

The big ferals walked away, their colours brightening as they crossed a patch of sunlight; Marlo swallowed the last of the roach and scampered after them. Jem worked his way down the peppermint's trunk and Cally trotted out from the fern; they waited for Kian to make some move but when he continued to sit, quite still, Cally asked, 'Are we going with them, Kian?'

Kian considered the wild cats, who had paused for some apathetic preening. 'Yes,' he said, 'we are.'

'What about the steely cobwebs? What about the poison?'

Kian watched Shyler tear a knot from his chest, Janshar brutally manicuring a puffball paw. It might be that the ferals were malicious, and held him in contempt; it might be that the pathologically pompous red tom intended stealing Kian's territory as soon as he discovered where it lay. But Kian was remembering the story told by the she-cat Tey, whose displaced mother had wandered forlornly until the forest dragged her to the ground. The story made him feel giddily sick and frightened, made his blood pump shallow as a bird's. Kian was a shiny cat lost in a perplexing, poisoned, cobwebbed unknown, and he was, for the moment, wretchedly thankful for the company of the wild ones. He looked down at the kittens and said, 'There's no poison or steel cobwebs where we come from, are there?'

'. . . No.'

'Well, that's why we must go with these cats. To get back where we come from.'

The kittens glanced at one another, bewildered, as Kian walked away; baffled into silence, they followed him out of the shade.

The Closing Storm

A CAT'S LIFE IS comparatively brief: if each of a cat's claws represents one complete journey of the Earth around the sun, then a healthy cat carries her lifetime's worth of journeys in her paws and has several claws to spare. The feline heart beats fast: although a cat spends quite two-thirds of her life dozing, cats live, nonetheless, a high-speed life. For a cat, a spin of the globe on its axis takes an impossibly long time, so each day is broken by necessity and naps into smaller, more civilised pieces, some of them lit by moonlight, some of them rosy with the sun. The six cats travelling through the forest made good progress, forsaking much of the sleep they might have enjoyed were they not pursuing intentions of their own. The transient life grates, however, on the feline nature – a cat likes to have her place and, having it, resents being chivvied from it. The constant movement, the lack of sleep and decent food and their perpetual wariness of the warriors whose ranges they were traversing soon rattled the nerves of the older cats, and made the kittens cranky. 'Why can't we stop for a while?' whimpered Cally, as the tepid sun made its voyage down, and Jem whined, 'I'm tired, Kian, I'm hungry.'

Janshar furled his ears belligerently, but Shyler came clumsily to Kian's rescue. 'You can sleep when you get home, Jem.'

'We eat there too, you know,' sulked the kitten. 'The woman gives us tea in the morning and meat at night. We weren't hungry, at home.'

Shyler had never heard of tea, and retired mystified; Marlo, who was walking the length of a dead toppled mountain ash, looked down from this kingly vantage-point and asked, 'Why does she do that, give you food?'

Janshar's lip crooked. 'Because they'd *starve* if she didn't.'

The ferals chortled; Kian whipped his tail. 'Where we come from,' he said, 'most cats are fed by humans.'

'*Why*, though?' The red cat stopped, eyes flaring in a shaft of sun. 'The sapien's the most selfish animal. Cats once made a bargain with him: we would cull his vermin in exchange for shelter and warmth. That was fair. But you say that, where you come from, hunting's just a game. If the sapien feeds you and you don't have to kill his mice, what is it that he expects in return? There must be something in it for him.'

'That's simple,' said Cally. 'They want to put their hands on our heads.'

The ferals gaped at her, incredulous; Janshar spluttered, 'What – *touch* you?'

'Yes. On the head, and on the back. It doesn't hurt – it feels nice.'

Janshar looked at Kian. 'Is this *true*?'

'I suppose . . .'

'How *creepy*!' Marlo jumped from the log and raced into the brush, haywire and afrizz. Shyler, ears up, watched the tabby go; he fanned his whiskers, bemused, and turned his eyes to Kian.

'Let me get this straight, cat. You don't have to hunt, you sleep when you want, you roam where you please, there's no poison or steely cobwebs, your meals come to you – all this in exchange for a tap on the head? Are you serious? That's your life?'

'. . . I suppose.'

The tom stared at the urban cat. 'That's unbelievable. I think that sounds . . . incredible.'

'I think that sounds *crap*.' Janshar strode to the nearest tree and, tiptoed and tail quaking, doused its hide with his corrosive smell. 'It's *undignified* for a cat to live like that. A *rat* leads a more honourable life – a *starling* is more wild! And there's one small but *significant* thing you've forgotten, Shyler, while you've been panting with such admiration: something about that life has turned them *not-tom*! Spin around, Jem, let's see you from behind – nope, nothing to be impressed about there! Something about that *incredible* little life has withered their nuts away!'

Jem glanced at Kian, distressed; Kian's hackles rose. 'You talk as if you were a tiger,' he snarled, 'but you're not a tiger, Janshar, you're a *cat*, an ordinary domestic cat, exactly the same as me, and I bet your ancestors lived the same as mine did, curled up by the sapien's door! How do you think cats came to this forest – do you think your forebears fell from the sky? *No:* a sapien brought you here, just as they've brought cats everywhere. You're not a tiger, and this isn't your jungle: you might be a wild thing but your queen's queen was not, and if you were given the choice, Janshar, you'd choose *my* life, not yours!'

'I don't think so, puss!' screeched the red feral. 'I'd rather be *dead* than not-tom!'

Scrote, Kian seethed: turd, malkin, mewler, dogshit. 'You've got a high opinion of your balls, haven't you? Tell me, Janshar, just how many kittens is it, that you've managed to sire?'

Their companions hedged away as the quarrelling cats yowled at each other. Kian stood his ground, deeply unwilling but prepared to fight. Cats detest being made to look foolish, and Janshar was clearly insulted to the core – yet he hesitated, glowering, unpractised and unsure; from the ferns came a gagging sound as Shyler choked on a blossom of glee. The red tom's paw was raised to strike and Kian crouched, hissing like an asp, and when Marlo squealed, both cats leapt involuntarily quite high into the air. 'Mouse!' shrieked the tabby. 'Mouse!'

A tiny native mouse had burst from beneath the striped cat's feet and was sprinting across the litter, its wheaten coat the colour of dry leaves, moving fast and smooth as mercury. The six cats dived after it, the standoff forgotten as they raced to snag the rodent beneath a flashing paw. The mouse accelerated desperately, tinny squeaks of terror piping from its throat, its hopes set on a fortress of gorse and tree-fern which was, for the cats, no more than three bounds away. In its final moments, the mouse was a credit to its plucky species: few beasts have ever run faster or more determinedly, or with such unlikely success, for it reached the bracken ahead of the cats and scurried into sanctuary – only to be snatched up by a vixen who, hunkered invisibly amid the fern, merely opened her jaws and let the luckless creature run into them. She swallowed the mouse in a gluttonous gulp and, fixing the cats with a merry but artful stare, said, 'You wanted that? Shame.'

'Calm down,' Shyler told the hysterically hissing kittens and Kian. 'It's only Fyfe.'

The fox flicked her feathery tail. 'Fyfe, not feline, who stopped the mouse.'

Kian had seen several foxes in his life, for they were a fugitive but not uncommon sight in the night streets of his suburb, but he had never approached or spoken to one. He had the cat's traditional cautiousness of the larger animal; Janshar, Shyler and Marlo, however, seemed to have little or none. Marlo snuck a paw out and dragged to himself a morsel that had dropped between the vixen's high-knuckled feet; Janshar and Shyler slumped casually down. The grey feral asked, 'What's been happening, Fyfe?'

'Well . . .' The fox rolled bloodstone eyes skyward, thinking theatrically. 'Just ate a mouse.'

'So we saw. What else?'

'Hmm. Hmmm.' Fyfe heaved a leaden sigh. She spoke to the cats with a toneless but faultless enunciation of their own language. 'Jauntied along to the farmhouse a dark and dark ago.'

'Oh yeah? We've just come from there ourselves.'

'See the dog?'

'Actually, we did.'

'Shirty, was he?'

'I reckon you could say he was.'

The vixen gurgled happily, the afternoon sun moving in mellow pools on her russet coat. 'Thought he might be. Poor dim doggy. Fox went down farmhouse when the moon was thin as a taddy's tail – sapien wasn't abouts, but woofer was, chained from neck to kennel. Chicks fluffy as furballs sleeping behind their wire, smell of the shell still on 'em. How could fox resist?'

'Fox couldn't, I reckon.'

'Got that right, red kitty. Chicken is a tasty bird. Chewed 'em all up promptly. Oh, he was barking and barking, dog was, strangling himself on that chain, I thought he was going to pop an eyeball, poor stroppy fella he is. It was a good dark's questing for the fox, all told. But I did feel sorry for the next four-leg who's meeting dog unchained.'

'That was us!' cried Marlo. 'We were next to meet dog unchained!'

'. . . And now fox meets you. Strange old world.'

The cats glanced peevishly at each other; the vixen's charcoal nose came down to sniff Cally, who bristled and bunny-hopped backwards, swatting the elegant snout. Fyfe cocked her head, charmed. 'Lucky dog didn't catch you, little one. Fox saw an empty kitty when the dark went, and one empty kitty's enough for this light.'

Janshar pricked his ears. 'You saw a cat that doesn't breathe any more?'

'When the dark went.' Fyfe sat, and used a tapered foot to scratch behind an ear. Spikes of her coat plumed in the air and coasted off into the trees. She trapped the flea between her toenails, and delicately ate it. 'Car got him.'

'Car got him?' Shyler repeated. 'What does that mean? Did a car take him away?'

The fox grinned, a pink pale tongue showing between pointed teeth. 'No, no! Oh, thicko kitty. Car *got* him!'

Kian, huddled against the shaggy trunk of a tree-fern, explained, 'The car went over the cat, and stopped him from breathing.'

The ferals balked, scandalised; the vixen pranced cheerfully.

'Shiny one knows!' she yelped. 'Car smoothed kitty! Emptied him right out. Been like that, oh, two, three darks. Gory he was, repulsive. He smelled, hmm, ripe.'

The cats ogled the fox and the fox stopped dancing and gazed amiably at them, her black-tipped ears tall above her head. 'Poor old fella,' she said.

'Was it a big cat?'

Fyfe's umber eyes went to Kian, detecting with ease his shape in the gloom. 'Bigger before he was empty.'

'. . . But, big?'

'Bigger than you. Bigger than any of you. Not as big as me.'

'Is he near?' Kian pressed. 'Would you show us where?'

'Near enough to near. Find him yourself, Shiny, fox has better things to do. What you fellas doing, anyway, rambling around with cubs in tow and getting yourselves chomped by woofers?'

'We're helping Shiny find his territory,' said Janshar.

'And red kitty's looking for a territory too,' said Kian.

'Hmm.' The fox yawned, suddenly and obviously bored. 'Well, do what you like. Follow the road thataway and you'll walk into smooth kitty: follow your nose and you'll find him mighty quick.'

'All right,' said Kian. 'I see.'

'Any more questions, Shiny?'

'No.' Kian felt it was something of an achievement, his first conversation with a fox, and he added shyly, 'Thank you.'

Fyfe blinked prettily, the breeze rifling through her coat. 'Fox's pleasure. I'll tell ya though, there's not much left of old smoothy to see. Ate most of him myself.'

The cats shrank backwards; the vixen gave a yip which resounded on the air and when the sound was gone so was she, not even scuff marks remaining to prove she had been anywhere. Kian, searching for sign of her, glimpsed the forest's ashy shadow perched high up in a tree; it stared coldly down at him, its gaze dabs of lucid light which made the cat's pupils constrict to hairline fractures, and he looked away. 'We should find the cat who doesn't breathe,' he told Janshar.

'Why should we?' The tom turned a frosty face to him. 'Fond of smooth cats, are they, where you come from?'

Kian stepped past the fronds and halted within reach of the feral's strike. 'A big empty cat,' he said, 'might mean a big empty range. This could be your chance, Janshar: you should go where he is, and see.'

Janshar's bronze eyes scanned Kian, pinched and thoughtful. Eventually he said, 'I was about to do that anyway. I'm just as clever as you, you know.'

Kian stayed stubbornly civil. 'The vixen said he's been flat a day or two already – we should hurry.'

'*We?* Do you think I need *you* to come?'

'. . . Of course not. But the kittens and I have to go that way, and we'll be safer if we travel together.'

Janshar was not stupid, but his reason, like that of most

cats, could be clouded by his ingrained vanity: he chose to hear Kian's words as repentance, a belated recognition of Janshar's vast superiority. The red tom had not, in actuality, relished the prospect of journeying on alone, but cats excel at instantaneously forgetting anything that it doesn't suit them to recall. 'I'll let you accompany me,' he conceded grandly, 'for the sake of the kittens. What about you, cat?'

Shyler, whose vanity had not been stroked and who saw, therefore, through shrewd clear eyes, swivelled his sights from Kian. 'I'll come along,' he said. 'Why not?'

No cat asked after Marlo's intentions, nor seemed to care whether the tabby followed or went away. He strayed after his companions as they traced their steps into the forest, but his sensibilities were stung. Jem dropped back to tread beside him and the tabby maintained a churlish silence under a battering of the kitten's chatter. Marlo was a grown cat entering his second winter and he found the indifference shown him by the older felines deeply offensive; he felt also that he merited better than the company of a babbling cub. Inside himself he understood that, although grown, he was young; he knew he could expect no deference from any cat until he had, perhaps, doubled his weight, an exercise in muscle-building that would stretch from this cold season to the next. Until then, he knew, she-cats would despise him and toms would threaten to thrash him. Marlo understood this, but railed against it in a torment of frustration. He would have sacrificed a paw to find himself, by day's end, miraculously and handsomely matured. He slumped along morosely, unresponsive to Jem's pranks and compliments and, eventually, to the kitten's own bleak silence. Instead the tabby listened to, though petulantly made no comment toward, the discussion between Kian and Shyler, who were weaving through the underwood ahead of him. 'I've never thought of foxes as friends,' the suburban cat was saying.

'They're not all as friendly as Fyfe,' the tom replied. 'She's a bit soggy in the head. But foxes aren't so bad. They're like us, you see, always on the lookout for cobwebs and poison. They're hounded by the hound, too – canine will break foxy's neck, if he catches him. Their own wolfbrother will pull vulpes from his skin. Fox, though, he just laughs at his barky kin, he likes to cause canine chagrin. Foxes are thieves and scavengers, and you wouldn't trust one as far as you could squirt, but the thing about vulpes is, they may be canis, but they'd rather be feline.'

Kian was amazed. 'Next you'll tell me you're rather fond of snakes.'

Shyler's foot slid into a dank puddle and he shook off with repulsion a skin of claggy slime. 'The snake hasn't got friends, and he doesn't want any. He's a dark and deadly shiver, is serpentes, but he's dumb – not like rattus, who's a devious scrote. Snake's only smart enough to think anything bigger than him must be foe. If he sniffs you getting too close, he'll bite, and the only thing he'll wonder while he's doing that is whether he can open his mouth wide enough to eat you as well. Don't ask directions from a snake, Kian.'

The cats walked on peacefully for a time. Soon after leaving the bowery with its scent of disappeared fox the travellers had met the road again, its rough edges sprouting tussocks of invasive pampas grass which soughed as they brushed by. It had begun to rain, however, and the cats had angled back into cover of the forest, where they wound through climbers and mouldering bracken and sheets of eucalypt bark. Janshar strode in advance of his company, Jem lagged at the rear. The air smelt swampy, sluggishly old, soupy with the oncoming storm; the sky was blotted by roiling cloud and the interior of the forest dimmed murkily. Birds hurried to the branches, arguing over prized roosts; minute insects, disturbed by the cats, hopped from the litter and pinged about, catching in the animals' hair. The cats lowered their heads against the rising wind, folding their ears to its chill. When the sky droned with sound, only Cally and Shyler bothered to glance beyond the canopy. A small silver shape was cutting through the clouds, its innards whirring urgently. 'Look,' Shyler murmured, 'a star.'

Cally chuffed. 'That's not a star, it's an aeroplane!'

'Well, it looks like a star.'

The calico kitten pondered the retreating craft, following it with her eyes. 'It looks like a star,' she mused, 'but it's a plane. We have lots of them – bigger ones, too – at home.'

The breeze was sleeking Shyler's whiskers to his face. 'What else do you have at home?'

'Oh, everything. Trains. Fences. Footpaths. Everything. Flowerpots, powerlines, telephones, all kinds of things. And once there was a jackhammer.'

'Do you have trees? Does the wind blow?'

'Of course! It's just like here.'

'Is it?' said the feral. 'It doesn't sound like it is.'

The kitten glanced at the tom. 'Maybe it's not.'

'Cally!' Kian, ahead of them, had paused, glaring sternly over a shoulder. 'You're being a nuisance. Go back and walk with your brother.'

Hurt, the kitten did as she was told, standing in the litter as Shyler, then Marlo, walked by; the forest flamed with lightning and she waited for Jem. Shyler turned on the urban cat, meanwhile, a knowing, mirthful gaze. 'I shouldn't ask so many questions,' he said, whispery as the breeze. 'Next you'll be thinking *I* want your territory too.'

Kian stared at the feral blankly. 'I don't know what you're talking about, cat.'

'No, I didn't think you would. You're a devious fellow, aren't you? We should call you rattus.'

'Rattus?' The black-and-white cat looked away. 'That would be wrong, not to mention unfriendly.'

Shyler's lip curved. He kept his eyes on the distant rump of Janshar, a marmalade flicker moving under the trees, a hooked red tail gliding over the soil. 'You're right,' he sighed, 'it wouldn't stick. You're actually a kind and thoughtful beast – I mean, just look at you. You're almost as eager to find a territory for Janshar as Janshar is to find one for himself. Any cat would think you were – well, *unselfish* – or something.'

Kian's tail swung. 'And?'

'And nothing. I'm just a little confused, because – well, I've never met a cat that wasn't selfish, and I don't believe they exist.'

Kian snickered; he watched Janshar negotiate the brambles, the red tom rapt in contemplation. 'I don't understand what you're talking about, Shyler – I think maybe you've eaten something bad. I'm as selfish as the next cat, I assure you.'

The grey tom turned his ears. 'That's good,' he said. 'I'm relieved.'

'. . . Do you think I'm right?'

'Right about the scheming of our grumpy friend?' The feral's attention caught on a moth and he tweaked it, expertly, from the air. 'How would I know, Kian? No one wears a collar here. I'm no cat's keeper.'

Marlo, trudging behind them, asked, 'What do you mean? Kian? What scheming? What are you talking about?'

Shyler spun, snarling. 'It's not your business, mewler.'

Marlo faltered and said nothing, but to himself he rumbled in the throat, and pricked the earth with his claws. Although there were three cats walking ahead of him and two kittens straggling behind, he felt isolated and somehow mislaid, an alien among his species. The feline's natural preference is to be alone and detached, but a cat also yearns for recognition: lacking the regard of others, a cat may as well not breathe. The most damaging insult ever hurled at a cat is the one that overlooks the cat completely. When rain began to fall in earnest, hammering the canopy and being channelled down primordial rivulets into the crow-black soil below, the rising mist suited Marlo's dreariness; when lightning jagged from the clouds and sheened everything blue he felt his hair lift, his flesh tingle as if scratched by talons of the sky. When the thunder exploded he quailed, feeling the planet beneath him tremble, wide-eyed and apprehensive but filled with a speechless admiration too: he wished he had been born a storm, which strikes with scathing power, which tolerates no disrespect.

The Dripping Canopy

IN THE DEEP of the night Cally opened her eyes. She sensed at once that the rain had stopped, although droplets were still plinking rapid as heartbeats from the points of fronds and leaves. When the storm broke, the cats, hating extreme weather, had taken hasty refuge in the underbrush, accepting the first poor promise of cover they could find and hunching into themselves disconsolately. Cally had sheltered below the hefty branch of a swamp gum which, though split from its tree, lay propped against the peeling trunk, clingy as an infant that won't wean. Kian was curled close to her, and Jem was draped along Kian's side. Both were sleeping soundly, Kian's soft pied face cradled in his paws. A short distance away, Shyler was bundled under the inadequate umbrella of a tree-fern; Janshar, more fortunate, had discovered a fur-lined hollow beneath a jutting rock. Neither the cats nor any other creature disturbed the draining forest and Cally yawned, wondering what had woken her. The moon, blanched as milk, luminated the darkness and painted the plantlife pewter; Cally smelt the refreshed sharpness of the air, scraped clean by lightning, and heard, very faintly, a dribble of water running from a height. The deluge had stopped only moments earlier, she guessed, and the nocturnal souls who would go hungry if they didn't forage were still deciding whether it was worth the effort, to set forth into the dampness from the comfort of a warm dry home.

A warm dry home: Cally shivered, the sheer air chilling her to the centre of her bones. Once, she had had a warm, dry home: in the lonely dark and coldness, that past seemed a long time gone.

Her listening ears heard a clatter of leaves and she looked out past the sloping limb, her chin tilting up until her jaws parted, exposing a row of spotless incisors. Her eyes showed no touch of their daylit amber, the pupils dilated to extremes in the tenebrous light. High above she discovered Marlo poised on the rough branch of a blueleaf, staring down at her. His tail gave a barely perceptible switch and he turned away slowly, anchoring his sights on the blueleaf's gristled trunk. Cally watched as he stepped carefully along the branch, each lowered paw tested for grip before weight was trusted to it, each step composed and executed with a painfully deliberate delicacy. The kitten, hypnotised by this aerial ballet, felt herself lulled and inclined to believe she had never woken at all.

Then, when he was a pace or two away from the trunk, the tabby sank on his elbows and hissed mutedly. Cally's drooping eyes blinked open and she saw what Marlo had been watching all along, and what had certainly been watching him. A bulky, dust-grey, wire-haired possum squatted at the junction of the trunk and Marlo's branch and was making no effort to improve its position, though it might have leapt for a loftier limb or raced agilely up the tree. It held its place audaciously, its ebony eyes fixed on the cat, predator and prey near-equals in size and armour. As Marlo teetered on the branch, his tail jerking to hold his balance, the possum opened its small round mouth and spoke in the complicated dialect of the natives, a language no immigrant species had ever troubled to decipher. Its words were garbled, its voice goblinesque; its own strong and flexible tail was wrapped assuredly around the branch and its mouth, opened, revealed two stained and daggerlike fangs. Cally tasted the peppery scent of the creature, its life of wood and water, flowerbuds and leaves. She puzzled how Marlo could have found himself in his awkward position on a sinewy branch, cornered by the nothingness behind him and the vacantness below, while salvation, for the brushtail, loomed sturdily at the creature's back – Cally had every youngster's faith in the infallibility of her elders, and it had never occurred to her that a cat might find itself on the wrong side of its quarry. So it shocked her to realise that Marlo was losing the contest in which he was engaged: one of his ears was lacerated, oozing blood dark as oil, and his banded coat was rumpled, rippling with spasms of agitation. The brushtail sat motionless, uninjured; its large eyes revolved and it looked at her, impassive as stone. She felt its gravity, and its loathing of her. It flared a paw, loosening the joints; on the tip of each slender toe arced a nettle-sharp, thornlike claw. It returned its gaze to the tabby and the animals stared incandescently at each other while, around them, raindrops continued to swell and fall.

At the heights of the blueleaf's branch, the wind blew steady and cold. The moonlit stands of eucalypt were jostling, mumbling ghosts. But for the grit of bark below his pads, Marlo could have believed he perched in empty air. He felt oddly suffocated, unable to draw a satisfying breath; his heart hurt when it hit his ribs. He knew his grip on the tree was unreliable and that his choice was to press his assault or abandon it in shame. A proud creature, aware he was observed, it was vanity that made the decision for him. He raised himself slowly, his ears folded safely and every hair bristled, making him look vaguely larger than was true. His sights were locked, now, on the possum, which continued to level at him an unswerving stare. A wintry yowl rose in the tabby's throat and the marsupial's ears rotated; it snarled diabolically, clashing its jaw. For a harrowing icicle of time the adversaries considered one another before the feral pounced forward with an unexpectedly unleashed ferocity, fast and vicious as a fiend. The possum reared and, as the cat ploughed into its stomach, threw itself on the tabby's back, its hind claws shearing skin. The cat screamed; jolted by pain he grappled with the branch but, unbalanced by the wraith around his ribs, lost his hold and slipped, slinging upside-down. He hugged the limb in a nightmare of terror while the possum plunged its fangs in him, stabbing his flanks again and again. The cat's screams rent the air around the struggling animals, swilled the haze of hair, spit and blood. They hung together for an excruciating moment before the agonised tabby pulled in his claws and let go.

Cat and possum tumbled together, the feline's instinct to right himself hampered by the weight of the creature on his back but working well enough for the cat to land gracelessly on most of his feet with the overturned marsupial boxed between them. The air was punched from the brushtail's lungs and it gasped, clenching its eyes: the cat, unthinking, seized the opportunity, driving his head under the marsupial's jaw and closing his teeth in its downy throat. The possum roared volcanically, raking the tabby's belly; Cally leapt forward, the carnivore blood shrill in her ears, only to be knocked sideways as Janshar dropped across the scene like darkest nightfall, and there was sound and scrabbling, and there was silence. The entire forest, it seemed, was silent; a bird burst as if detonated into the sky crying *wheep, wheep, wheep* as it went; when it had gone, the silence returned.

Marlo stood panting, his head bowed. He shook ruby drops from his eyes. 'I could have done it myself,' he wheezed. 'I didn't need your help.'

Janshar was lying on the possum, pinning its carcass to the earth. To ambush a full-grown brushtail was courageous, but the tom felt no admiration for what the undersized and inexperienced tabby had done; rather, he wondered distractedly why any cat should be so determined to stop himself breathing. 'Look at you,' he scoffed. 'You're in pieces.'

Beads of dribble plopped from Marlo's chin to the dirt; his eyes were glossed with pain. Nevertheless he stood steady, instinctively unwilling to betray any sign of weakness and invite the observation of competitors or predators. 'I had his throat – I had him in my teeth. I could have done it.'

'Assuming your head was still on your neck, numbnuts.'

The tabby trembled. He glanced at Shyler, Jem and Kian, who had woken to the screech of battle and been astounded spectators to the short but savage drama. His gaze reeled drunkenly to the marmalade tom and he stumbled, just slightly, on his four feet. 'But I could have done it. Janshar. Say I could have done it.'

Janshar only stared at him blandly – a cat parts with few compliments and will have none dragged out of him – but the tom's reticence was satisfaction enough for the torn and bleeding tabby, who shuffled into the brush to inspect his injuries. His appetite dulled beneath his pain, he did not wait to feed off the opened corpse; when he had brooded on and tended his wounds he fell into an enfeebled unconsciousness, shivering in a nest of leaves. While he slept, his companions ate their fill of his conquest, the ferals crouching possessively over the kill, grumbling at each other, Jem, Cally and Kian forced to wait, anxious with the smell of it, fretting they'd inherit only bones. The marsupial meat was dense and hot and there was enough of it to leave them all feeling leaden, sated and sleepy as the sun began to rise. Kian lifted his face to the shafts of light spearing the canopy, the coils of steam charmed up from the composting ground. Purring, he let his eyes close, nestling a stone in his paw. Dry and fed and feeling through his whole body the unbroken beat of the Earth's croon, this was the first moment of real contentment he'd had since finding himself in the forest, stripped of his collar and depressingly far from home; the first time he felt content, he realised, since the last time he saw the old woman Ellen. No cat, however, can worry with enthusiasm when he is lazing on a bloated stomach and Kian let the haw slide over his eyes, his thoughts winnowing away. He fancied he glimpsed feline shapes flitting through the treetops, the shades of cats who lived in this place and called everything in it their own; hungry cats drawn by the ursine smell of brushtail, who touched the ground like feathers and drifted soundlessly between the sleeping travellers, picking up the remains of the possum and carrying into hiding this rare and precious prize. Kian, his moon-white chin resting on the swarthy earth, dreamt of the forest's spirit, saw it looking through his eyes, felt its force like a spangling heat in his core; in the dream he ran on dexterous paws, prehensile toes clutching a branch, solid but nimble inside a woolly, smoke-grey skin. Tree and star and sky were his world, laced at the edges with leaves. He heard himself speak a language he didn't know and the spirit in the forest answered him, its sound the same as trees uprooting, as rocks and mountains rousing themselves from an epoch of inertia. A cuckoo's calls woke the cat to confusion, the essence of the marsupial flowing swiftly away. Give me your strength and fortitude, he begged, as the warmth poured through his paws; give me all that you don't need any more, your courage to live gallantly until the end.

Later in the day the cats stirred themselves, flexing and preening and sniffing hopefully at the place where the possum carcass had been. Marlo stood tentatively, his muscles taut, his injuries no better for his recuperative sleep. His copper coat was tattered, hanks ripped from it and querls of clamminess haloed around each weeping laceration. The other cats stayed clear of him, for he smelled of blood and marsupial and, lame with discomfort, it was not difficult to predict what would happen to him should a dog sift his odour from the air.

Janshar, though, had been buoyed by the slaying; Kian watched him splash his mark over nearby trees and gouge his claws into more, yanking chunks of bark from the trunks.

He saw that Janshar had stolen the triumph, had pirated the possum's conquest from Marlo and taken it on as his own; he saw that, to the red tom, the tabby's role in the slaughter had become that of insignificant fool. When the cats moved into the undergrowth Kian hung back, pondering how to use this latest surge in the tom's egotism. Eventually he weaselled close to the feral and asked, 'How many possums have you taken, Janshar? Quite a few, I suppose.'

The rangy tom cast him a lofty glance. 'You'd think so, wouldn't you, but that was my first.'

'Really? But you were so skilful.'

'Yes, I know.'

'You didn't hesitate, in the face of tooth and claw.'

Janshar sighed, wearily tolerant. 'What can I say? Some of us are worth admiring, and some of us are not.'

'It's true. You wear the stripes of a tiger. It suits you, to live in the forest.'

Marlo stumbled forward, protesting noisily. '*I* fought the possum, not him! You saw that, Kian!'

Kian paused in dark-blue shadows, aware that Janshar's eyes were on him. 'I did,' he admitted. 'I saw it. You put yourself in danger, Marlo.'

'Yeah, I was brave –'

'No, you were foolish. That beast was your better – you're lucky Janshar came to your rescue when he did. Remember you only have one life, Marlo: you can stop breathing just once.'

With that he walked on, his paws greased with sticky mud, stalked by the bitter glare of the tabby, trailing the delighted red tom. Callousness comes naturally to a cat, yet Kian ached with shame. In putting his own concerns first he was doing, he knew, as a cat must always do; in safeguarding his territory from the plunderous designs of Janshar, Kian was ensuring he would bring himself, and with him the kittens, home. Nevertheless he felt only sick when Shyler spoke from the shade. 'What a slippery cat you are,' murmured the unkempt feral. 'What a slippery, sneaky feline.'

Marlo, lingering where he'd stopped, let his gaze drop listlessly as the big cats faded into the trees. Cally and Jem paused to wait for him; Cally said, 'Kian didn't mean to hurt your feelings, Marlo. He gets angry at us all the time – doesn't he, Jem?'

'He sure does.'

'He gets worried, that's all.'

Marlo didn't answer; he sat in the stodgy litter, twisting to lick fiercely at a wound. The kittens watched, interested. 'Does it hurt much?' Cally asked him.

The tabby snuffled. 'Nope.'

They watched him contort, tug a tangle of hair, rip it ruthlessly from his coat. Jem said, 'Do you know what I remembered, Marlo, when you fought the possum?'

The feral straightened, glancing incuriously at him. 'Nope.'

'I remembered those big cats, Whit and Loke. Remember when we saw them brawling? When you fought the possum, you were just like them.'

The tabby's ears lifted. 'Really?'

'Yeh!' Cally jumped up. 'You were!'

'You were, you were!'

'What was it like, killing the possum?'

'How did you do it, Marlo, what was it like?'

'Tell us, tell, tell!'

So the tabby shook the dirt from his coat and rambled with the kittens into the forest, graciously and elaborately relating to the youngsters the gory details of the fight. His resentment was soothed, but cats forget nothing, and it pleases them to hold a grudge: Marlo did not intend forgiving what Kian had said to him.

In the early afternoon Shyler swore he detected the scent of an amorous female and although the ferals admitted it was cold weather for a she-cat to be feeling friendly, they were not inclined to quibble the point; the smoky tom trotted away through the scrub and Janshar hesitated only long enough to say, 'Keep to the road, Kian, we'll catch up with you,' before dashing through the bracken after the feral. Marlo mewed plaintively to see them go, unsure what to do; in the next instant he too had run off, the tang of blood floating in his wake, an overturned beetle kicking in its shell. Jem loped into the ferns after him, but returned when Kian called his name.

Cally stared down the corridor of waving fronds and weeds that marked the path the wild cats had taken. 'Will we be all right by ourselves, Kian?'

'Of course,' he answered dauntlessly, and licked her grubby face. 'There's nothing in the forest meaner than a calico cub.'

But Kian was remembering the dog and talk of poison and the mystery of the steel cobweb; the knowledge that he was a shiny cat made him flick his tail edgily and he felt, like ice on his spine, the frigid crystal gaze of the forest. A graver threat than these, however, lay in cats themselves, in the potent ferals who claimed the land and took dangerous offence to trespassing. Kian sighed, wondering how long it took to woo a she-cat – he had to admit he had no idea. Nudging the waiting kittens he said, 'Come along.'

Pebbles and Birds

THEY DID AS JANSHAR told them and kept close to the road, although not so close that they slipped into the open and could be distinctly seen. Kian did not want to encounter another wagtail whose outrage would betray their presence to every creature under the canopy. The sunshine following the overnight rain had steamed the forest temperate and, despite his apprehension, Kian found it pleasant, sauntering through the pampas and onionweed that sprouted by the road. Scattered about, stuck in the dirt, were tiny things whose familiarity made his heart pang – a bright-blue plastic hair-comb, the wafer-thin sole of a tennis shoe, a flotsam of cigarette butts, a crushed aluminium can. Jem and Cally soon abandoned their caution and began to skylark in the weeds, competing exuberantly in their efforts to impress him. They were still young, and brainless for it, but he thought they had changed since coming to the forest. They exercised a judgement that had been sharpened by the ceaseless change around them, by bushland as alive as any breathing thing. They did not squander energy, now, by taking fright at every movement or noise: they scarcely glanced upward when there came the bone-breaking fracture of a stringybark branch, and Kian, black-eyed with his own alarm, wondered at the degree to which the siblings had become, already, wild. They were adapting to the quirks of the forest and leaving him, befuddled, behind. Well, he thought, what could a cat expect: he had been born and bred a metropolitan cat and lived his entire five years that way and, until he had seen it with his own eyes, Kian had been unsure what a forest actually looked like.

If memories of their suburban life were blurring for the kittens, to Kian the past remained pristine as a droplet of sunshower. In the past he had controlled a territory and that tidy rectangle of rather ordinary land had been, for him, a source of pride and purpose and significance; now, separated from his range, he felt stripped of worth and racked with the craving to retrieve it, to *return*. This craving was persistent, niggling as a marchfly: Kian knew that, if they had to, the kittens could adopt the forest as their own and feel no loss in doing so, but that his own heart would soon break if he were forced to stay, if he could not, one day and finally, go home.

'Kian? Kian!'

He looked up dazedly. 'What? What, Jem?'

'Why is grass green?'

'Well . . . because green is the colour of cats' eyes.'

'See!' cried Cally. 'I told you. What about the breeze, Kian? Why does it blow?'

'That's easy. To brush the dust from your whiskers, kitten.'

The siblings raced away, crashing through ivy and thistle. Kian watched them, his white paws finding a path between the weeds, but, inside, he coasted away. He remembered his life before Jem and Cally, a life of sunstruck footpaths and of sleep so deep he would feel himself sink through the surface below him, would wrestle the drowsiness like a cat swallowed by a lava sea. And then some sound would save him, a door rocking on its hinges or the squeal of the brakes on a car, and he would wake in a flash, his head jerking up and his eyes blazing open, the pupils flooding and contracting to motes. It would take him a moment to realise who he was and where, and Kian sighed to think how safe he must have been then – safe enough to forget himself.

He could not say how fond he had been of the old woman, Ellen: he had tolerated her as well as any creature endures an occasional harmless interference in its life. For the most part she existed as a peripheral figure in his world, less than secondary to the neighbourhood cats and to his own engaging company. When he was hungry, however, she became his fixation and obsession, he would twine between her ankles bewailing his state, beseeching her with suffering eyes. She was slow in everything she did, and he could smell the acrid age in her. She annoyed him sometimes, stroking his coat's electricity to life, petting him until he was driven to scratch, pestering him with her presence when he wanted to be alone. She would speak her droning language when he preferred silence, and startle him deliberately when he was concentrating on a bird. Frequently he had been forced to describe to her his displeasure in some razor-sharp way. Mostly, though, Ellen had respected his privacy, seeming to understand his need for freedom and solitude; she saw that he inhabited a world she was not invited to enter, and she appreciated the forays he made into the tamer world of her own. She gave him meat and fish and cheese and made space for him on her bed, and in the colder weather she would put a rug before the heater which was his reserved and princely place. She had a variety of cooing names for him, none of them his true name, but he recognised them anyway, for no feline can be defined by a single word or tone. He allowed himself to be shut inside on inhospitable nights and in his boredom he could be overcome by bouts of luxurious affection for her, draping himself against her chest, the flesh of her face wobbling under the power of his purr. Sometimes he could not resist reaching out a paw to tenderly touch her cheek; she would stroke his throat in return and he had often thought, in those moments, that a cat could do worse for himself, that she was not so bad.

This opinion took a battering the day she set a box on the

floor and he thought it must contain something of interest to him: peering over its lid, he'd almost vaulted out of his skin. He could not say for sure how Ellen was responsible for bringing the kittens into his territory but he was absolutely certain she was to blame, and on the spot he decided to most rigorously punish her. For days on end he sulked, coiled under the bed and lashing out malignantly if curiosity drove the kittens to investigate his hideaway. Ellen tried to tempt him out with milk and cubes of liver, folding painstakingly to her knees to seek him among the suitcases. He had stared stonily at her, his tail frapping disdainfully. When she left the room, he'd snuck into the open and gobbled her offering.

'Hey, Kian?'

'Hmm?'

'You know how puddles shine? How come they do that?'

'So a cat can see himself, of course.'

Jem swished his black tail merrily, and fled.

What had possessed the old woman, to make her do such a thing? She had never before behaved with such abominable heartlessness. He did not bother wondering if he'd done something to deserve the affront – Kian knew he had not. When he'd eventually emerged from under the bed it was with an air of persecuted martyrdom and he'd stalked the boundaries of his territory sullenly, refreshing his marks, ignoring the catcalls of his hated speckled neighbour. The kittens were irresistibly drawn to him and he swatted them hard whenever he could, crouching to blast into their faces a hiss that could shred concrete. From a prudent distance they told him how they'd been the last of their litter left in a cage in a bizarre, bustling and noisy place that smelt warmly of dough and rotten produce. In this place had been bundled fruit, vegetables, kittens and pups, and ducks both headless and otherwise; the people who had thronged there had been encouraged to pinch, prod and squeeze them all. The sibling cubs had huddled in a corner of their cage, their tiny paws slipping through holes in the wire, the sun's heat heavy on them and the scent of their mother fading even as they pined for her. Ellen had stopped, and stared at them. 'It wasn't our fault,' whispered Cally.

'Shut up!' he'd spat, the first words he spoke to them, and it gave him some rueful amusement to realise that, from that moment onwards, they never had. Kian was, essentially and to his sorrow, a benevolent cat, as well as being lazy: rage demanded an energy he could never successfully sustain. The kittens, for their part, adored him without mercy, and their desire to be with him, to imitate him, to look to him for answers and vie for his attention, all of this was flattering to a cat, and difficult to dislike. He assumed an avuncular attitude toward them, playful and tolerant, reserving always the right to be suddenly bored, and walk off on his own. While they were young the kittens were, to Kian, a vexation, but not much worse than that. The matter of Jem would become pressing as the black cub grew older – Kian's mind was only slightly relieved the day the tom kitten was carried from the car sleepy, and not-tom – but, for the present, both cubs were small and impressionable, and easily cuffed about.

'Kian?'

'Yes, Jem.'

'What about rain? Why does it fall?'

'It falls . . . well, to coax a cat from his sleep.'

'Oh. Know what? I'd rather stay asleep.'

A cat notices everything, and in the long stretch of baking weather which followed the kittens' arrival Kian noticed the old woman becoming slower than usual; lying on her chest with a paw buttered under her chin, he felt her heart flutter and heard the restive churn of her blood. An ancient instinct came to life in him and he shied from her when he was able, his skin crawling under her touch. When the weather cooled and the leaves turned yellow, when the nights grew longer and morning scattered dew on the lawn, even then he felt her body struggling with the effort it had become, to keep the fluid coursing in her veins.

He remembered the last time he had seen her because he'd been napping on the roof of the car and she had woken him by plucking gently on his ear, a custom he disliked. She had with her the wicker basket, the deep bowl of which was another of his favoured resting sites. The pale bones of the basket smelt of food that had been inside it, the grassy pulp of oranges, the antiseptic aura of supermarket ham. Kian had jumped from the car and lain on the driveway after she'd driven away, the loury scent of engine oil massing in his nose. He had dozed beneath the lacklustre sun while the broad leaves of the plane tree floated to the ground around him, graceful and wide-winged as swans.

She had not come back. As his mealtime passed he paced in agitation, finally sitting on the doormat and staring crossly down the street, straining his ears for the putter of the car. Jem and Cally were locked inside the house, both of them grown gangly now, having survived their first half-year, and he could hear their hungry bleating as evening aged the sky. Kian settled on the mat and slept there, snapping awake several times in the night. The lights of cars would whiten the garden and rush on, attentive to their duty. By morning, she had still not returned.

His repulsive neighbour was pampered with a dish perpetually filled and Kian helped himself to its contents, stepping away on haughty legs when the speckled cat rounded a corner and discovered him. The kittens were active inside the house and he heard some plaything harried across a room. Later they were quiet and he sprang to a windowsill and saw them sleeping in the embrace of each other. He rattled the window's frame, but the lock was turned tight. He walked the building's perimeter, testing handles and putting his weight to doors. He was an escape artist, locked out. At sunset, awake again, the kittens wailed and scrabbled at the glass, crying for him.

Three more days and nights passed, and Ellen still did not come. Jem and Cally, shut inside the airless house, were quelled: sometimes he would see them through a window, lonely hollow-flanked creatures wandering the length of the empty hall. When the man arrived and opened the front door the kittens were nowhere to be seen but the smell of them billowed from the rooms, making the man bark and growl.

Kian had seen this man before – he was an unmistakably large and hairy creature whose fleecy face Ellen would touch with her lips on the infrequent occasions he visited. He was a human whose voice was rough as a dog's and the pitch of it, in the past, had always prompted Kian to disappear; to hear Ellen and the man conversing was to hear a goldfish argue with a wolfhound. Kian understood a sprinkling of sapien words but the man would soon teach him more: *getoff, pissoff, fuckoffcat.* The man arrived in a car that farted smog and he carried into the house a bag of clothing, trailing everywhere he went the reek of his body draining its liquids and sloughed-off flakes of skin. The kittens were immediately banished from indoors, recalcitrant Jem hurled out by the scruff of his breakable neck. Within days the house and its surrounds were fuggy with the man, his smell slithering beneath the door like a slug on a wet midnight. Through the window Kian noted that he slept in Ellen's bed, snuffling in a lump of blankets that would slide gradually to the floor. The man was absent for much of the day and some nights he did not come home at all. He threw out food for the cats when the idea occurred to him, gritty hard-edged kibble that the fussy animals had often rejected when it came from Ellen's hands. Now they ate it fast and gladly, their eyes darting up constantly, leery lest he approach. When he had been at the house for as many days as Kian had claws, the man came home with boxes that he kicked and tossed the distance between the car and the front door. Kian, sitting on a windowsill, watched without comprehension as the man packed Ellen's possessions into these cartons; Cally, napping in the flowerbed, turned her ears when she heard the jingle of the bell inside her ball and Kian saw the fluffy object get thrown into a crate. The next afternoon both the kittens and he were locked inside the final box, lured close by uncooked hunks of mince that they did not, in the end, get to eat.

Kian's lime eyes had been watching the forest, watching the kittens, watching for something worth making into a meal, but he had been seeing little. Now he returned to himself and saw Jem, ahead of him, drinking from a rainpool, the sound of his tongue touching the water like diamonds tinking off each other. Cally had run up a tree and was shredding bark with her claws, a chipper madness agleam in her eyes. Kian could remember every cranny of his territory, could feel in his feet the shape of its pebbles and hear the call of each resident bird. He did not know for certain what had become of Ellen: he remembered her toiling body and he had his suspicions but he could not explain why the car and the basket, which had never breathed in the first place, should have disappeared as well. As for the man and his eccentricities, Kian was utterly nonplussed as to why the creature had felt the need to put three cats in a carton and leave them in a forest.

'Kian. Kian, look. A bird that limps. I'll catch it.'

The jet kitten dashed through the pampas; the lame aviator took to the air. Thwarted Jem watched it go. 'I wish they couldn't fly.'

'Look at your sister, running away.'

The kitten's citrine eyes blazed, he took off at a gallop. Kian's thoughts hurried home. The curious behaviour of Ellen and the man was, in truth, of no concern to him. The territory was all-important: if, when he returned, Ellen had returned too, he fancied he would be quietly pleased; if, instead, the man was still lurking, it would be a simple matter to evade any box that happened to appear. Cats learn, and rarely fall for the same swindle twice.

But returning to the territory was what mattered – returning there healthy along with the kittens, whom he felt honour-bound to deliver, but unescorted by any feral who had the strength and the will to wrest the territory from him – a feral like blackguard Janshar. It had become, to the lost cat, immeasurably important that he extract himself from the conniving company of Janshar. Kian had a groundless confidence that, if he could rid himself of the red tom, every obstacle destined to confront him on this odyssey would crumble away with ease. Once unshackled from Janshar he was home, safe, free.

Soon, Kian promised himself: soon. Soon, if I keep walking, I will be home.

'Kian!' Jem called. 'We found it!'

He had forgotten they were searching for anything. Lifting his nose he could smell what he could not yet see, the piteous but useful thing. The kittens were inching toward it and scrambling away. Kian pushed through the weeds and stopped by the road. There, attended by flies, lay the remains of a cat – the unlucky cat of whom the fox had spoken and partaken, the cat who could not breathe any more. A cat who had relinquished its territory and existence under the wheels of a speeding, belching vehicle: beneath the stench of the dead animal Kian's excellent senses detected the odour of the sapien, slimy across the dirt like worms after pouring rain.

Spinning Leaves

THE FERALS DID NOT meet the urban cats until late that night, long after the whistling bats had dispersed through the sky and the big spiders who made their homes in the earth had gone prowling, their tiptoes fondling the ground. Cally had seized a mouse in the early evening, and Jem had stolen half of it from her; Kian had made do with moths and a tailless lizard. The refugees had nested where the fetid smell of feline corpse was damped by the brawny scent of tree-ferns, and fallen asleep together in a pile of fur.

Jem woke abruptly, startled to find himself nose to nose with Shyler. The tom sniffed the mouse on the kitten's breath and his fine whiskers quavered, brushing the younger cat's forehead as he stepped away. The forest was very dark, the moon a smear behind a pallid shroud of haze, a fog that smudged the edges of everything, making this cold world opaque and shallow. But for the rasp of a solitary cricket there was no sound – not even leaves nickered against one another. Cally was awake and sitting tensely; she turned an ear, but not her attention, in the direction of her brother. 'We have to stay here,' she told him, 'and be quiet.'

Kian, Janshar and Marlo were hunched on their elbows some distance away, squinting through the weeds at the clot of cat remains. The cats were well hidden in the pampas and grass, and Jem had to sharpen his sights to find them – it was Kian he saw first, the white of his coat shimmersome as hail. Shyler crept through the foliage to join them, burrowing into the weeds. 'This whole area belonged to him,' Kian was saying. 'You can smell his marks everywhere.'

'He's still making his mark on it,' observed Marlo. 'He stinks.'

Shyler chuffed, and the knavish ferals knocked skulls; Kian disregarded them. 'This is your chance,' he urged Janshar. 'It's a good territory, and you should take it.'

Janshar shifted his weight, the weeds rustling around him. 'Yeah,' he said. 'I will.'

Kian waited, but the red tom did not move. He sagged, instead, a little heavier against the ground. Shyler and Marlo swapped wry looks. 'Go ahead,' Kian prompted.

'In this lifetime, Janshar –'

'I said *I will!*'

The tom struck out, smacking Marlo on the head; Kian

hissed scoldingly, scanning the still canopy. 'Quiet! Let's be quiet, shall we? Janshar, is something wrong?'

'*No.*' The marmalade feral was sullen, turning his face away.

'Well, good then. You can do it – off you go!'

Janshar's tail twitched the grass. For several moments he said nothing, ears folded irefully. Finally he grumbled, 'That's easy for you to say, Kian. It's not *you* who has to go out there.'

'Ha! He's scared!'

'Shut up, Shyler! You're right, Janshar, I don't have to go out there, I've already got a territory, but –'

'So how did you get it?' Janshar's glinting eyes glared into Kian's, angry and confused. 'How did a raggy malkin like you get a territory? You couldn't fight a cat like Whit or Loke, so how does a *not-tom* keep a range?'

The pampas crackled as Kian dug his claws into it, but he managed to keep calm: he reminded himself of Janshar's sheltered upbringing within the clowder, protected by she-cats and elderly toms. It was to be expected that such a cossetted animal would be overawed by many things. 'It's different, where I come from. For most of us, our territory is the place where we grow up. We don't have to brawl to earn it, we just age into owning it. We'll fight an intruder if we have to, but fighting's a last resort.'

'What do you do, then, if you don't brawl?'

'Spit, growl, biff, yowl – you know, the histrionics. One

cat or the other runs off and that's usually the end of it. It's mostly just menace – bluff, I suppose.'

Shyler snorted. 'What a pack of pussycats.'

Janshar whacked the iron-grey tom, who retreated into the grass; to Kian the red feral seethed, 'You hiss and spit and gripe and bluff, but *you* tell *me* to fight!'

'Of *course* we bluff!' Kian winced with exasperation. 'Why would we battle, when there's a less risky way? Only a crazy cat *wants* to fight!'

Their bickering disturbed a nightjar, who swept from its perch and flew grimly away. The cats stared watchfully into the canopy, glimpsing through its torn holes a bleak, wafting sky. They searched the black branches and shadows, struggling to see through the night. Wild cats, they knew, were nearby, moving carefully but unswervingly in on the vacated range, cats that would soon smell the bivouacking travellers, would soon stare down on them. Kian thought feverishly, concentrating his wits; he cursed himself for not devising a plan earlier, he who had always prided himself on his gift for strategy. Desperately he reminded the tom, 'You killed the possum, Janshar. If you could do that, brawling a cat will be *easy* –'

'Hey!' Marlo bridled. '*I* killed the possum, not him!'

'All right, you both did –'

'No, I did!'

'Shut it, mewler.' Shyler cuffed him. 'No one cares.'

The tabby glowered, whisking his tail, but the bigger cats

noticed neither him nor his rage. Janshar, who'd lived his life unquestioningly convinced of his talents, wondered for the first time what exactly those talents were. Kian looked up as a frugal rain began to fall and saw clouds flow like oil beyond the cat-claw moon, the night's waxy eye turned the colour of wet stone. Marlo was staring darkly in the direction of the carcass as if psychically aware of something the rest of them were not – Kian knew the young feral sensed nothing, then was nervously unsure. The kittens, soundless behind a screen of fern, had squeezed close to one another, agate eyes blinking, ears pivoting restlessly. Rattled, the red tom spluttered, 'There's vicious cats in those trees, Kian. Cats more vicious than me. I won't win, if I fight one of them.'

The admission must have almost throttled such a popinjay as Janshar, and in reply Shyler cawed like a crow. 'You'll never get a range if you're gonna be sooky about it!'

'Little kitty!' Marlo jeered. 'Are you scared, mewly mew?'

Janshar jumped up, lunging at them. 'I'll brawl with you scrotes any day!'

'Get out there and fight, grimalkin!'

'Squirt on you, doghole!'

'Quiet!' Kian yelped. 'Be quiet!'

The ferals subsided into the grass, snarling spitefully at each other. A shadow moving amid the leaves made them sudden comrades again, raising rounded, worried eyes. Something was definitely alive up there, and the travellers dug deeper into the meshing of grass. 'I've got a plan,' Kian whispered, 'but we need to be quiet. It won't work, if they see us here.'

Janshar dragged his gaze from the trees. 'What is it?'

'Well, it's bluff. If the cats out there believe you're fierce enough to thrash them, they won't want to fight you. You need to make those cats think you're strong: if you can do that, you'll get the range, and no cat will dare try taking it from you. You make those cats think you're strong by fighting a mean cat, out there, where every cat can see you – and by winning.'

The ferals looked at him, deadpan. Shyler said, 'That plan might have worked, Kian, except for one tiny flaw. If Janshar fights a mean cat, he's going to get his spot kicked.'

'I'm warning you, craphead!'

'There's no flaw.' Kian stepped between the ferals. 'The plan will work, Shyler – there's no flaw. Not if *you* fight Janshar, and lose.'

The grey tom's eyes went to him, black and glitterless; not even a whisker moved. 'You're very funny, cat.'

'Oh, come on, Shyler! You're a tough animal! They'll be impressed, out there, if they see Janshar thrash a cat like you! *We'll* know it's not a real fight, you won't be shamed –'

'It won't be real, I'll flay you just by accident –'

'Janshar, *shut up!*'

'Squirt on you, glandbag.' Shyler glared at the lanky tom, his pupils refracting red and green. 'Not in a hundred lives,

Kian. What's in it for me? Nothing. What do I care if Janshar wants a range? I don't. Not a bit.'

'Coward.'

'Janshar!'

'Sniff me, knot.'

'Shyler!'

'No!' cried the smoky tom. 'Never! All a cat has is his dignity, Kian. If you want some cat to fight Janshar and lose, do it yourself.'

'Him!' Janshar hooted. 'What's impressive about him? Scrawny shiny housecat, frightened of everything – I might as well fight that she-cub!'

Kian bristled, infuriated – but inside himself he crawled. There was no point trying to defend himself, they'd listen to nothing he'd say. Not for the first time since casting his reluctant lot with these ferals, he wondered if he wasn't going quietly but violently mad. He could flee the scene, he knew, and a voice inside urged him to do just that, but running has a tendency to offend and provoke: Jem and Cally, left confused in his wake, would doubtless bear the brunt of the ferals' irritation. He glanced at Marlo who, still suffering the effects of his possum-inflicted injuries, sat bunched tightly, small against his pain; for all his noisy bluster, the tabby was far from being an admirable sight. Kian thought, again and wistfully, of his beloved home territory, and of his creeping belief that Janshar was plotting to steal it. Surely the madness lay in imagining such a thing – or was it, in fact, the only thing he saw clearly? He sighed, his gaze straying past the pampas to where the feral lay ground into the road, and he knew that this opportunity, once wasted, would never come again. 'All right,' he breathed, throwing doubt and prudence and every care into the wind. 'All right, let's do it.'

The red tom hesitated, resentful, unconvinced, but he could not back down now without appearing a coward himself. 'This is a stupid idea,' he told the refugee, 'and I don't reckon it will work. I'm only doing it because neither of these meatheads thought of anything better. Fuzz yourself up, then: if we're going to look like halfwits we might as well do it properly.'

'I don't *have* to fight,' Kian answered him coolly. 'I've already *got* my own territory. *I'm* only doing this as a favour to *you*.'

The feral grunted; he trod from the tangles of grass into a patch of open forest, his chin lifted boldly, his tail straight and high. He strode to the nearest tree and scored its bark with his claws before swinging aside to leave his musky scent. Kian, low in the grass, watched the performance, deeply depressed. He looked at Shyler, who folded scrappy ears: 'Sorry, cat,' the tom said.

Janshar, standing alone in the clearing, announced, 'I mark my claim – this is my range now! I'll shred any cat who tries to take it from me. Does any cat want to try?'

The forest answered with silence. A raindrop collected

on the point of a frond. An insect droned its wings, sending shivers down feline spines, and then the silence resumed. Kian and Shyler exchanged glances, their ears straining to catch sound, but nonetheless it took them by surprise when a blood-curdling caterwaul soared down from the canopy. It was a piercing, mocking scream, a buzzard of sound that swooped across the clearing and sheared through the trees, pulverising the raindrop that glittered on the fern. Jem and Cally shrank from it, and Marlo went wild-eyed. The cats saw Janshar wrestle against the instinct that commanded him to run. There was a mighty feral lurking in the branches and the creature would, at any moment, follow its gauntlet-screech to the forest floor. Shyler nudged Kian's shoulder. 'Go on, cat. Hurry.'

Kian gripped the dirt, insanely hopeful that, in this crucial moment, something incredible would occur to rescue him from this ludicrous scene. Nothing did, and in an instant his powerful legs sent him sailing over the spikes of the pampas, a live voltage clad in black and white. His forepaws hit the earth in front of Janshar, scuffing leaves and tiny stones; his head slung down and his ears went flat as he opened his mouth to roar. He reared, flared a paw of switchblade nails, swept the weapon forward and smashed Janshar across the eyes.

The blinded tom shrieked with fury and while he was vulnerable Kian attacked, boxing the feral with a string of thumping blows. Janshar fought his way from under them and Kian glimpsed the tom's shocked eyes, huge and incensed. In the beat of time allowed him Kian gasped, 'It has to look *real* –'

Janshar either failed to understand, or understood a little too well. He sprang into the air and came down like a howling boulder, sprawling on Kian and crushing the urban cat to the ground. Kian scrambled, his vision smothered by the tom's bulk, his chin grinding into the soil. 'Get off me!' he squawked; he could feel the feral's claws nicking skin from his body and heard a manic gurgle rise inside the animal's chest. Kian kicked and squealed, choking on hair, unable to see, unable to breathe: desperation drove him to twist his neck and bring his teeth together in the tender flesh of Janshar's groin.

The red tom bucked, wailing like a bird, and Kian rushed across the clearing, his ears slick with terror, catching sight of the kittens sitting mesmerised behind the fern. He felt his flesh snag on Janshar's claws and spun from beneath the feral's grip, stumbling as the soaked leaves skidded away. 'Stop!' he yipped. 'Let me go!'

Janshar loomed above the overturned cat, and swung a bladed paw: his claws raked Kian's mask, leaving long bleeding streaks down his nose. Kian wriggled frantically, his hind legs guarding his belly, his paws grappling for the feral's eyes. The air that surged between them was blurred with fur and muck; from behind gritted teeth Kian pleaded, 'Stop it! You'll give me an abscess! Stop!'

'Didn't I say this was *my* range?' Hot breath blasted from the wild cat's lungs, sweeping through Kian's hair. 'I'll *kill* any cat who tries to take it from me! Did you hear me say *that*, shitball? *Kill!*'

Kian, distraught, sank his claws into Janshar's head and hauled himself close to the feral's face. 'I said *stop!*' he gasped. 'You're hurting me! That's enough, Janshar, let go!'

The tom retaliated by driving his hooks into Kian's chest; incarcerated in each other's grip the cats glared, their noses touching. If Janshar saw outrage in Kian's eyes, what Kian saw in the feral's lit a fear hot as fire. He did not see a cat he recognised – there was no conceited marmalade tom. That foolish animal was gone – Kian had a weird sense he'd been slaughtered – and his frame had been filled by a predator who stood at the lofty zenith of the food chain, from which place all other beings were competitor or prey. Here was a hunter whose every thought revolved around the catch and kill, a beast who offered up a short, carnal, ruthless life, a life soaked in fluids and splintered with bone, in exchange for supremacy over every living creature. Kian, recognising the thing he fought, went slow and weak with dread. Janshar hugged the cringing cat close to him. 'I'll take your eyes,' he growled, almost kindly, into Kian's black ear. 'Hear me, kitty? I want your eyes.'

The sharp red face pushed nearer, images of itself reflecting in the refugee's petrified eyes. Kian, on his back, felt cold soil slithering beneath him, saw sentinel trees, shambling ghosts, mantled in light from the stars. He glimpsed the forest's shadow watching calmly from the branches. He kicked lamely, drained by terror, his mind smogged crimson with fear, and only distantly did he notice a paw snaking past the feral's shoulder. The paw felt for the feral's eyes and, finding one, unsheathed its talons and dug in.

Instantly Janshar released his hold on Kian, who raced into the trees without looking back. Jem, hitched by a claw to the storming feral, bounced and jerked as the big cat scuffled to shake free. The dark kitten was lithe and speedy and almost invisible in the night and when his claw tore through the tom's eyelid he sprinted for the ferns, every hair on him flying upright but confident that the feral would and could not follow. He heard the sound of cats rampaging, bolting through the scrub, and knew there were too many for them all to be his allies. Above him, in the blackness, branches broke and leaves dropped and birds rang alarms. About him, in the thickness, stones rolled, bark snapped, and rodents ran for cover. Behind him Jem could hear the triumphant bulling of Janshar, the tom bawling ownership of the dead cat's vacated domain. Ahead of him Jem could see nothing but more of the covenish forest. He galloped on, his golden eyes dark as char, wondering where he was going and if he would be found.

The Wakeful Forest

JEM COULD NOT know it, but he was not the only cat to have lost his companions. When Kian stopped running he found that only Shyler had run with him and that Marlo and the kittens were nowhere to be seen. The grey feral stood panting in the darkness, staring back over his rump in the direction they'd come from. His ears were up, his tail lashed, his coat was silvery with the moon; he turned shining eyes to Kian and chirped, 'How good was that!'

Kian scowled, sitting down to inspect his injuries. One of his eyes was watering and tufts were loosened all over his coat. Three long lacerations were stinging on his nose. In the distance he could hear the noise of the disordered forest, the agitated swill of the birds, the splenetic garble of marsupials, the twanging bark of a fox; this offended chorus was split down the middle by the depraved screams of a warrior feral.

The forest itself, giant ash and flaking manna gum, towered in the darkness, creaking like bones; the blades of their leaves were polished by moonlight, which pooled in the hollows of their bark-strewn crowns. Shyler frisked joyfully from tree to tree, kicking up moss and wadded leaves; finally he spun himself into the dirt, clutching spread-eagled to the ground. 'I can't believe that stupid plan worked!'

Kian spat out a snag of hair. 'It wasn't a stupid plan. The plan worked. Janshar was stupid.'

'Well, at least you got what you wanted: I reckon he's forgotten about your territory!'

'Hmm.' A knuckle of cold satisfaction scraped Kian's spine, a wintry sense of pride in his own cleverness. 'Good riddance.'

Shyler leapt to his feet and stared into the forest, tail swishing vehemently. 'I still can't see the others,' he reported.

'Did Jem get away?'

'I guess.' The tom searched the shadows. 'Why wouldn't he? We should have told him the plan, that you and Janshar were pretending – idiot malkin, he thought you needed help. Dumb mewler. Brave little scrote, though.'

Kian held an elegant silence. He'd expected Shyler to have seen how serious the bogus battle had become, how badly in trouble Kian had found his hapless self; he'd expected the tom to find the botched charade profoundly amusing. But Shyler clearly didn't realise that the pantomime had turned real – probably no cat had except Jem, who never knew the thing was supposed to be a sham. The humiliating fact remained that Kian had been saved by a kitten, but at least this fact was not commonly known. Jem could be told his interference had been both inconvenient and unwanted, and made to feel guilty for meddling. The threadbare scraps of Kian's self-respect would patch together for appearances' sake, and that was important, as appearances are. Inside himself, however, there was nothing that could disguise the craven truth, and Kian was shattered to know it. Being rescued from the hound by the ferals had been embarrassing enough; to be delivered by a youngster from the clutches of another cat was more, much more, than any feline with pretensions to nobleness could bear. Janshar in his cruelty had been correct: Kian was only a scrawny housecat, neither brawny nor brave. He might as well, he thought miserably, have been born a flower. 'Let's rest here a while,' he sighed. 'Maybe they'll find us.'

The feral flopped into the leaf litter, rolling happily about; Kian lay down somewhat gingerly, his belly ticked with wounds. He was exhausted, having hurtled fast and far in an effort to put distance between himself and the demented red tom. In their harum-scarum flight through the forest he and Shyler had crossed the road – Kian could still feel the bite of its gravel on the pads of his paws. According to the call of the Earth, recrossing the road had been necessary and Kian was glad to have finally done it, it made the Earth beat a little stronger for him – but he did not know if the same tune was sung for Jem and Cally, and whether they had any hope of finding their way home or to him. On the frayed fringe of his awareness he heard Shyler say something about foraging a meal but Kian shut his eyes tightly, morbidly downhearted. His entire body ached, from the black peaks of his ears to the white flag of his tail. He hated the forest and everything in it, and he yearned for the comfort of his house, his basket, his chair. A bead of drool gathered on his chin and glimmered invitingly – Shyler had to fight the urge to swipe at it, but his kittenish exhilaration died away as he watched the urban cat sink sadly into himself. Kian was a thinner and tattier animal than the one he'd been the first night Shyler met him, when he'd stood with some courage before the she-cat Tey and the inquisitive water clowder. The tom propped in the leaves, shaking off their debris. 'Do you have far to go,' he asked, 'before you reach your territory?'

'Yes, far.'

The feral drew himself together, tucking his paws to his chest. In general cats have little regard for how another creature is feeling, but Kian's profound sorrow made the tom edgy: of all the emotions a wild animal knows, unhappiness is the least familiar, and Shyler had no clue how to react. He tried, 'Would you like me to sing? I know some songs.'

'Thank you, but please don't.'

Kian felt the tickle and shook his head, flinging the jewel

of dribble away. Shyler watched him stretch a leg and pull it close, unable to get comfortable on the moist forest floor. 'Cat,' he said.

Kian said nothing; his tail twinged.

'Maybe you shouldn't wait for the others. Maybe you should go.'

Kian's eyes opened a fracture and he regarded the feral, who leaned conspiratorially forward and spoke rapidly into the dark.

'Forget the kittens. You're not their mother. You'll be better off without them. You'd travel faster, you'd attract less notice. No cat would blame you, Kian. And then, when you reach your territory, it will be *your* territory – all yours.'

Kian looked down. 'It is mine.'

'Is it? But you said yourself: where you come from, a range belongs to the cat that grows up on it. Wasn't Jem growing up on your territory? Doesn't that mean it's his territory too?'

Kian licked his teeth, his tongue rasping past his fangs. A minuscule insect was rambling over his toes, astray on the snowy expanse of his paw, and he watched it turn and turn around. While Jem was still small, no more of a threat than this clueless gnat, Kian had avoided thinking about the problem that was him. 'Sometimes,' he said, 'where I come from, male cats will share a range.'

Shyler's lip jerked. 'Share? What is share? No cat I know ever willingly shared a thing. You've just had a fight with

Janshar, because you know that's so. Janshar and I were banished from the clowder, because every cat knows that's so. One day Jem will want ownership of what's yours, and then he'll challenge you. You'll win the first few skirmishes, you'll knock him back in his place. But the day will come when little Jemmy's in his prime but the cold nights you've seen have dug into your bones . . . When he challenges you that day, that's the day he'll win.'

The breath from Kian's lungs stirred the wings of the insect, making it veer in circles. He had seen it happen, had met cats to whom it had happened, cats forced to live furtively in territories they had once commanded, sad degraded animals pushed to the boundary by the strength of some newcomer. Jem was still a young cat, prey, for the present, to the dominance of his elders, but he'd shown a fiery potential, attacking Janshar as he'd done. Kian tried to imagine what sort of cat the dark kitten would grow into, how hot ran the blood of his unknown kin. He glanced at Shyler, whose black-lined eyes reflected the opal moon. 'That's the day you'll wish you'd left him here,' the feral murmured, 'when you had the chance.'

'. . . The cubs wouldn't survive in the forest.'

'Yes, they would. They're young enough to learn wild ways. If you like, I'll promise to leave them somewhere Tey will find them. They'll grow up safe with her, in the middle of the clowder. She will teach them what they need to know. And they'll be all right.'

Kian's gaze lingered on the tom; the insect continued to dither. The forest was finally quietening and Kian heard the breeze stroke the canopy. He remembered his first evening in the scrub, standing before the clowder on the bank of the creek; he remembered the suspicion that had come to him, that the ferals would swiftly kill the kittens if given the slightest chance. 'Why are you saying this, Shyler?' he asked. 'What do you care what happens to us?'

'I don't care,' answered the feral. 'Why should I care? I'm just trying to get rid of you the quickest way I can. You're wood-headed, Kian, you couldn't survive out here on your own. You'll be latched onto me like a flea forever if I don't shake you off somehow.'

Cats, unlike dogs, are not skilful jesters, and Shyler was suddenly worried that he'd said everything wrong. He got to his feet and stalked back and forth through the darkness, staring hard at the ground. He batted a seedpod and sent the kernel pinging into clumps of olive bracken.

'You should go home to the warm house and the full bowl, Kian. Home to where the mouse is a toy and there's houses in rows and you can sleep all day. You should go home to the old woman who pats you on the head. That's where you should be. It's not right, a cat like you walking around out here. This isn't your proper life. You're just not . . . uncollared enough.'

Kian dropped his ears. He had not cared to mention it but days and nights later it still seemed strange, to move without the accompanying jingle of a bell and metal tag. Shyler had paused beneath bending fronds, and was looking at him.

'You should go,' he said. 'You should go home as fast as you can. Travel light. Travel alone. Take this chance. No cat would blame you.'

A barn owl skimmed over their heads and through the stand of gums, angling its immaculate wings to thread the narrow gaps. Kian watched it flap away, staunch and severe on its mission, living out its solitary, intensive life. He turned an ear to Shyler when the tom, concerned that he might be giving an overly benign impression of himself, grimaced and spoke again. 'I mean, that's just what I think. Do whatever you like, I don't care.'

Kian said, 'The old woman – Ellen – I don't think she breathes any more.'

'No? Well, everything that breathes stops doing it one day.'

Kian's eyes went to the gnat, which was toiling, now, along his leg. Shyler sat, his tail curving to his lean rump. 'I'm not certain,' said Kian, 'but I think I'm right.'

'. . . Well, then.'

'I haven't told the kittens. I imagine they will be distressed.'

There was a scuffle in the underwood and the cats looked up alertly, seeking its source. 'The owl,' Shyler suggested. 'It's found something.'

Kian sighed, and looked down at the insect. 'I'm hungry,'

he said. 'I can't remember what it's like, not to be hungry. To be so well-fed that I could walk away from a meal without finishing it, leave the plate for the snails to clean. Ellen kept a box of kibble in a cupboard: if I was peckish at night, I could work the door open and scoop food from the box with a paw. Some nights I did it because I was bored, just for something to do. I never thought I'd find myself here, with possum bones and lizards in me, forgetting what it's like to feel fed. How do you bear it, Shyler?'

Shyler did not know what a cupboard was, and he had never heard of lock or door. Hunger, however, was something he knew well. 'Being hungry is part of being alive. Sometimes I'm awake, sometimes I'm asleep. Sometimes I'm hungry, other times I'm not. I decide these things for myself, and if I choose wrong there's only me to blame – but, if I sleep well or eat well, the pleasure is all mine. That's the way life is, here: my thoughts are with me, I am my own cat. Maybe these are wild ways – not your ways, Kian.'

'No.' The urban cat looked at the feral. 'They're not wild ways. They're feline ways, that's all. I am my own cat, also: I have never stopped thinking about myself.'

The feral's whiskers fanned. 'Then you must have thought about leaving the kittens. Going home alone is your best hope of getting home at all. A cat is beholden to no animal but the one inside his skin, Kian.'

'Yes.'

'The kittens are young. Young enough to learn. Young enough to forget.'

'Yes, I know.'

'What makes you think you can get them home, anyway? How do you know you can keep them safe? Maybe it's *better* for them to stay here. And what's going to happen if you *do* get them home, and find that this Ellen doesn't breathe? Who'll care for them then? Who will fill their stomachs? Can you, Kian – as well as filling your own?'

The gnat somersaulted down Kian's leg and dropped to the forest floor lugging a wispy, sable cat hair. Kian turned the feral's questions over in his mind, sniffing their unknown scent. He had given no thought to the practicalities of the future and he wondered if he'd done that deliberately. It made his hackles lift a little, to think of the man's hand reaching out to Cally. The slate tom waited for an answer, staring at him; abruptly the feral jumped to his feet and paced vexedly. A moth teetering across the clearing was swiped impatiently from the air; the tom cried, 'Do you even understand what I'm saying, cat?'

'Of course.'

'Because I'm trying to *help* you, Kian.'

The refugee glanced up, chuffing dryly. He could smell the feral's frustration, felt it buffeting the air. 'You've got nothing to skite about, Shyler,' he said. 'You should stop showing off. You're not half as selfish as you pretend to be.'

Shyler stopped pacing. 'No need to be insulting,' he said. 'I'll keep my opinions to myself, if you're going to be nasty about it. Come on then, cat, get up: I reckon that owl found something squeaky, and where there's one squeaker there's always more.'

So Kian got to his weary feet and the cats prowled into the night scrub, watched as they went by a large chequered wattle-bird who had woken with the din of the territorial brawl. She would not stay where cats were hunting and, opening forked cream-flashed wings, pushed off the branch and struck the air. Smaller and less belligerent than her male counterpart, she made no comment as she swooped the cats, her strong wings and tail shaped like a crossbow, her flight fast as an arrow. She was a blossom-chaser, and should by now have flown for the warmer inland. A blade-cold winter would soon seep into the forest and its chillest nights would leave snowflakes in their wake, and crusty carapaces of ice. It would be a hard time to be a bird in the forest, especially a bird devoted to sunshine who had lived her pert life in the wattle, its round yellow flowers echoes of the sun itself, but the wattlebird knew she would not have to endure this approaching onslaught. Birds are beloved of nature, and nature is kind to them. One night soon she would pleat her wing with her beak and not wait for dawn. Meanwhile, she was most aggrieved: she dived through the nighted forest, cutting the air that lay thick as quicksand over the road, tilting for the low ground where morning would arrive soonest. Within moments she had flitted into invisibility, oversoaring but failing to notice, from her blue-black altitude, a tabby cat and a calico cub who stood beyond the road's brink and who, for their part, did not bother looking up to her.

Squall

AT THE HEIGHT of the battle's commotion the tabby, forgetting his pain, had hared into the forest with no reason for running other than a surge of hot-headed exhilaration. He had vainly assumed the others were following and been somewhat crestfallen when, slowing, his lonesomeness was revealed. He had scanned the undergrowth, focusing his senses for feline, filtering through the cacophonous protests of the unsettled forest. His many hurts had come back as he stood there, the sickening tug of sealed wounds breaking open, the throb of blood beneath swollen injuries. He shook himself and stood tall, attempting even when solitary to seem healthy and carefree. His acute ears detected a woebegone whimper and Marlo had trotted toward the road, where he'd found Cally, her amber eyes staring, hunkered in the weedy centre of the trail; with the forest rearing massive on either side of her, white with swampish fog, the kitten had looked the smallest and most misplaced creature ever to have walked the Earth. As soon as she saw him she'd scuttled close and asked, 'Where is Kian?'

'I dunno. He ran. I can't find Jem and Shyler, either.'

Cally glanced about uneasily, belly to the ground. 'What shall we do?'

Marlo, recognising nothing of the surrounding scrub and feeling far from the security of his clowder, was disconcerted, and hesitated. 'We should stay here. We must have run too fast. We'll sit and wait for them to catch up.'

Cally watched him lower his haunches to the dirt. The forest behind them rattled as something tumbled from its perch; from a mushy trough came moaning that made the kitten fold her ears. Long ropes of ivy dangled and swayed, probing the ground, searching for grip; the wind burled down the treeless channel of the road, driving before it a chattering of leaves. 'I don't want to stay here,' the kitten whispered. 'Let's go back and look for them.'

Marlo wasn't certain that he wished to stay either, but, eluder of dogs and slayer of possums that he was, he could not let himself be ordered about by a kitten. 'No,' he said trenchantly, 'we're staying here. You don't know the forest like I do. It's not safe for cubs. We'll stay and wait here on the road.'

Cally had stared at him, her coat roughed up by the breeze.

The moon glowed on the feral, highlighting his sturdy outline, sparkling on the spike of each hair. 'Kian says never to trust a road,' she told him. 'Cars go on roads.'

'. . . Yeah, so?'

'Cars empty cats.'

Marlo slapped his tail, surly. 'A car wouldn't get me. Do you think I'm dumb? I've seen cars before – they're slow. They're fat and slow and knotty. They're morons. If a car tried to get me, I'd run. I wouldn't even have to run fast, and it still wouldn't get me.'

Cally's eyes gleamed: without another word she walked off the track and into the scrumbly bracken. Marlo watched her go, and when she'd disappeared in the welter he had gazed at his paws and then at the moon and into the trembling forest. The night was very cold, and he fluffed his coat around him. He felt a little ludicrous, sitting lone and priggish by the road. Any passing creature might think he was strange. He'd gazed into the scrub but could not see Cally, the grass through which she'd woven closing densely in her wake. He couldn't hear any cats – apart from the breeze and the knocking leaves he could not, now, hear anything. He grizzled crossly and charged after the kitten, dots of soil scattering from his toes. He found her hiding in a hollowed-out eucalypt, frightened by his noise and speed; she'd skipped from the shelter when she saw it was Marlo, and he'd been flattered by her happiness. For all her determination, Cally had not tacked deep into the forest – when he looked behind him, Marlo could still see the road. 'Did a car come?' she asked.

'Nah.' The tabby honed his claws on the dead trunk. 'I remembered old Tey would make a fuss, if she knew you were roaming round alone. If a car had come, it'd still be climbing trees trying to catch me. It'd be gnashing its teeth and going hungry tonight.'

Cally scampered after the feral, who had leapt a clump of wilting fern and was sauntering away. 'Have you ever seen a car, Marlo?'

'Yeah, heaps. How many have you seen?'

'Lots. There's lots and lots where Kian lives.'

The tabby changed the subject. 'You live there too: it's not just Kian's home, you know.'

'I know, but it doesn't –'

'Kian's a bully. He wants everything his own way.'

'– but it doesn't matter. I know it's my home too. Kian just likes it more.'

The feral looked at her. 'How much do you like it?'

Cally screwed up her nose. 'I liked it lots at the start. The old woman was nice to me.'

A stone slipped under Marlo and his tail was dunked in the puddle beneath: Cally waited while he shook and licked it clean, and neither of the cats noticed the wattlebird fly overhead, intent on lower ground. Even as Marlo wiped off the worst of the water, the cold wind began to harry the fog, chasing it into troughs and mutilating its hems. Marlo straightened and, with a final insulted jerk of his tail, limped on. 'If the old woman was so nice,' he said, truculent, 'why did she leave you out here?'

'It wasn't Ellen who did that, it was the man.'

'They're all the same to me,' sniffed the tabby.

The wind was blowing in Cally's face, making her squint. 'I think the man wants us to stay in the forest. Why would he put us in a box and bring us here, if he wanted us to come home?'

Marlo only grunted, his thoughts still ministering to his tail. Cally moved closer, lifting her voice above the breeze.

'Maybe, when we get home, the man will put us back in the box and bring us out here again. I don't know why Kian hasn't thought of that.'

'Kian thinks he's superior,' announced the tabby: cats are nothing if not vindictive and the feral had been carefully tending the grudges he'd gathered against Kian, unable to forget the many snubs and denigrations he'd endured. Any chance to avenge himself against the hoity-toity urban cat was being impatiently awaited by the younger animal. 'He's too busy thinking about himself, that's why.'

'He hasn't even asked if Jem and I want to go back.'

'. . . What, don't you want to?'

Cally, like all cats, could see perfectly in daylight and superbly in gloom, but in complete darkness saw no better than do most other creatures; when the moon was cloaked by heavy cloud the kitten lost sight of the tabby and found herself talking into a swathe of featureless night. 'I like the forest,' she said. 'I think the forest is the right way for cats to live – the real way, the wild way. But Kian wants us to go home, and I have to do what he says.'

'Why should you have to do what he says? He's not your mother!'

'No, he's not. But I know Kian better than I knew my mother. I can't remember what she looked like, but Kian's face is in my eyes. I can't remember the scent of her, but the scent of Kian is mine, too, because he curls up with me and keeps me warm. When my mother was gone and Jem and I were alone, Kian gave us a place to be, he shared the old woman, he shared his comfy chair. Kian is the cat who's teaching me to be a cat, and if he says I must go home then I must, because he knows more than me, and he's never been wrong. So I'll follow him if he wants me to, but I think it'll be for nothing in the end, and he'll be disappointed. Because I don't think Ellen breathes any more.'

Marlo had never previously encountered such stalwart loyalty but his feline sensibility reacted to the concept as it would to something repulsively putrid, and pushed him adamantly away. Cally hurried on. 'Do you remember the black cat, the thin one, in the clowder?'

'Givench? What about him?'

'Well – he smelled, didn't he? He smelled tired. He

smelled as if part of him had already stopped breathing. Kian's old woman smelled that way.'

The cloud coasted beyond the moon and the tabby saw lights appear in the kitten's eyes. 'So? Kian would know it, if she did.'

'But I don't think he does . . . at least, he's never said anything. But if I'm right, we'll walk all the way home and Ellen won't be there – only the man, and he hated us, he hated everything. I don't know what Kian will say then, I don't know what he'll do. He'll have travelled so far to find her, and she will still be gone. His heart is going to break, I think.'

Marlo stared at the kitten, the rising wind scudding his coat. He tussled briefly with the predator's inclination to tamper with the hopes of another, but the opportunity to sully Kian's pious reputation was far too perfect to let go. 'Kian's not going home to the old woman!' the tabby chortled. 'He's going home to his *territory*! Don't you know that?'

Cally cocked her harlequined head. 'But to Ellen, too. She belonged to him. When Jem and I came to live with him, he was angry – he thought we might steal her.'

'He was thinking you'd steal his *range*, you mean! He couldn't give a rat's arse about the sapien! She could be on the moon, for all he cares! Kian's going home to his territory, and that's all he's thinking about. Trust me: if you were a tom like me – or even a not-tom, like him – you might understand.'

Cally gazed at the feral, her long white whiskers blowing

back to her face, gripping the ground against the force of the breeze. 'No – no, that's not right –'

'Oh yeah? Have you ever heard Kian *say* he's going home to Ellen?'

'. . . No . . .'

'Me neither. He hardly even mentions her. But I *did* hear him yabbing about his territory when you and Jem were eating the bandicoot, and I *did* see him pretending to fight Janshar, because he knows how important a range is to a cat.'

'. . . The fight with Janshar was pretend?'

'Of course it was! That's why it was so hilarious when Jem jumped in to help. I nearly hacked up a hairball!'

Cally sat down, struggling to make sense of what the moon-dappled feral was saying. 'Kian's going back to his territory,' she breathed, examining the statement as if it smelt interesting. 'He's not going home to Ellen.'

Although a cat, Marlo was not intrinsically ruthless: the sight of the little kitten sagging with disenchantment filled him, suddenly, with grumpy regret. 'Kian's a cat,' he said petulantly. 'He has to do cat things. What's wrong with that?'

The kitten glanced up, starlight flitting across her face. 'Nothing,' she said, and it was true that she could find no good reason for feeling so disappointed and deceived.

The wind had summoned its strength and now, in the thick of night, blasted the forest with the drama of a hurricane; the rawboned eucalypts unwound burly ribbons of bark which rode the wind like sails. Pockets of the forest were infested with non-native trees that had thrived since the time, an age earlier, when their forebears were given freedom to sprout at will: the last discoloured leaves on their comatose branches were stripped by the ruffian wind and sent flying. Decaying banks of ground-litter were pulled apart and spattered in hunks against tree-trunks and stone. The leathery leaves of the natives kept their hold but the trees themselves leaned and shuddered, every passing gale tempting them to apathetically lay down their lives. The squall streaked through the forest on freezing sheets of air, driving before it a rubble of twigs and weeds and blackened leaves, crushing beneath it foraging creatures caught offguard, slinging water from shallow creases and smearing it into the ground. Cally and Marlo cringed as the whistling force hit them from the side, the wind kickering from their coats a haze of hair. These fine strands gusted away, the squall spiriting them through the forest higher and faster than any cat could travel, dashing them disdainfully through the netting of canopy and casting them, with a billowing flourish, toward the starry sky.

The wind dived like a whale and the cat hair tumbled down its cresting flank, spinning chaotically until, the gale having powered on its destructive way, it fell freely, a silky, dun-coloured rainshower. It slipped between branches and surfed the trunks of cabbage gums before meandering to the ground. A spike of Marlo's agouti coat came to balance on the point of a small, black, feline ear and the ticklish touch of it made Jem shake his head quickly, reflexively, so the tabby-barred strand flew away. Two tiny eyes were watching the dark kitten and his movement made their owner, a hump-backed echidna, rustle its bristles pugnaciously. The scorched bushfire sound of this pleased Jem, who showed his appreciation by enthusiastically swatting the roof of the monotreme. The echidna snuffled grouchily. It did not fear the young cat who crouched nearer, now, to inspect its refined snout, for it wore a needled suit of armour and its feet were awesomely clawed, but it was in no mood to be made the poked and prodded object of feline entertainment. The monotreme abhorred intemperate weather and hankered to escape the gale; the kitten formed an obstacle between it and its burrow, and it was not pleased by this delay. It opened its mouth, a slit as fine as fishbone, and spoke with some length and indignation. Jem slumped on his haunches and listened ardently, understanding not a word.

When the black kitten had eventually slowed his flight from the scene of the territorial battle, it hadn't unduly troubled him to discover that not only was he alone, but he had no idea where he was or which direction to take. He wasn't frightened of the forest – he rather liked it. He was giddy with the excitement of his attack on Janshar, his first-ever brawl and one from which he had emerged, more or less, the victor: the thought of standing unaccompanied beneath unseen eyes did not spook him as it might have, before he'd fought the feral. In the absence of any cat to impress or obey, Jem's kittenish tendencies had sprung to the fore. He'd transformed into a black-eyed bronco, bounding, flinging himself in circles, leaping like a cricket into the air. He pulled down moths with arcing swipes of his paws and ate their bodies messily, the creamy slime that filled them rolling in globes down his chin, the torn wings evading him, fluttering away. When the wind swooped through the forest he had raced ahead of it, his body a phantom of speed. The gale ran faster than he did and he stopped as it blasted over him, his hair blown so askew that he felt, for an aching instant, turned inside-out. Jem adored this wild world: he wished he could somehow relinquish himself to it so he would never have to leave. It grieved him to remember how close the chance of staying had come, and how it had been thrown away.

Jem had hardly been able to believe his eyes when, hiding behind the fern with Cally, he'd seen Kian leap the pampas to challenge Janshar's claim on the empty cat's range. Until that stunning instant Jem had thought Kian was determined to return to his sedate life in the suburbs. Clearly, however, the bigger cat had changed his mind, or perhaps he had always been fooling them all, for he'd fought Janshar fiercely, seriously intent on securing the territory. And Jem, behind the fronds, had been thrilled, for if Kian won a range and stayed in the forest, surely he and Cally could stay too. When he'd realised

Kian was losing the contest Jem had not hesitated to jump into the fray, desperate to see his hopes come true. But then, of course, Kian had run away, and with him went flying Jem's dream.

Jem did not feel any resentment toward Kian, who had abandoned him to his fate beneath the wicked claws of the red feral. No cat asks for assistance in a battle, and none would expect gratitude for providing such a thing. The kitten's disappointment, however, itched like a wound. The chance to live forever in the forest had come so tantalisingly, so *cruelly* close, but now it would never return. Jem knew that Kian, ashamed in defeat, would absolutely insist they return to the suburbs. And he knew that, when they eventually reached home, he was going to find his old existence a grindingly boring thing. Out here, he had been touched by wildness: back there, he would have no choice but to become a cat like Kian, satisfied with a little life. His tail whipping, Jem had looked up to the treetops and past them, to the low-slung moon. He could feel his heart pulsing inside his willowy frame, the brightness in his eyes, the quickness in his feet. A self-assured and clever cat might have made, at that moment, a decision about its destiny, but Jem, just a kitten, was neither of those things: though riddled with a surly sense of having his wishes denied, he could not invent for himself a future which sidestepped going home with Kian. Disgruntled but resigned, he had shambled into the darkness, bleating for his missing companions; he had taken only a few steps before discovering the echidna and being immediately cheered, every trace of sulkery forgotten from his mind.

The echidna had shouted at him almost before Jem recognised it as something alive: it had a pipsqueak voice and its incoherent shouting was not loud, but the kitten heard its fury. He knew the animal was trying to drive him away but a cat and his curiosity are never easily parted and Jem sniffed all over the creature's swarthy body, peering into the seedlike eyes, snuffing down the fragile ears. The echidna's snout creased and tilted, following Jem's face as if resolved to jab him, given the chance, promptly in the eye. Each movement of the monotreme's head made its spines rasp like sand. Its paddlelike legs peeked from a thicket of fur and thorns; its fleshy underside, protected by this fortress of prongs, was safe from all but the most impervious foe. The echidna abused the kitten in a language of clicks and tickings, the sounds as roughly musical as pebbles cascading over a waterfall: Jem could not understand it, and did not think to try. Swollen with bravado, he stepped back to inform the monotreme, 'I could eat you, if I wanted to.'

The creature's head swayed, its eyes shining with the night. It spoke again, rapping out chipped words. Jem patted its brow. 'Lucky for you, I don't want to.'

The echidna's spines rippled and Jem quickly withdrew his paw. He stared, entranced, as the monotreme sank steadily into the crumbling earth, apparently without the least effort on its part. It sank like a flower in water, almost lazily. Spurts of dirt shot from beneath it occasionally, but these were the only sign of disturbance in the soil. The echidna descended, infiltrated, it simply seeped away. The kitten watched, mystified, and very soon found himself looking at a nondescript smudge on the ground, a stain which resembled a freshly-buried echidna in no respect at all. Jem hissed through his teeth. He felt the need to make the monotreme aware of its good fortune in crossing the path of a cat who did not, at that moment, happen to be hungry – he did not want it thinking that felines were easily dealt with, that a cat could be defeated by that tricky coat of spines. But it would feel odd, addressing a blotch, so Jem shook himself and left, trotting into the scrub to search for Kian and Cally and the wild cats, content once more with the world.

Far off through the windswept forest, where leaves continued to drop from the trees and a troop of flying-foxes were unfurling jagged wings, the red feral Janshar stood on a branch of his territory's tallest tree and saw his dominion spread below him, every twig of it his for as long as he had the might to defend it. Far from him, beyond a span of forest so badly pummelled by the gale that it still tremored, Cally and Marlo hunched side by side at a sliver of rainwater, licking up the coldness and watching one another from the corner of an eye. Through the bushland that surrounded them ran the road, a ridge of earth rising between parallel trenches carved by tyres. On this ridge grew a wilderness of weeds and native grasses, a miniature ecosystem populated by miniature beings. On the distant side of the road the forest was quieter, for here the squall had not been so severe; deep in its damp gutters a sea of honeysuckle had swamped a stand of tree-fern, ropes of vine wrapping the trunks like anacondas, and behind these choking ferns scrounged Shyler and Kian. Between them they had so far turned up nothing more appetising than a huntsman which Kian had immediately gobbled, coughing on the legs. The grey tom was growing peevish: since wolfing down his inadequate share of the brushtail, an entire night and day earlier, he had eaten almost nothing. Dawn would arrive soon, bringing with it prime hunting conditions, and Shyler was jittery in anticipation of eating well or not at all. When he saw Kian standing with his nose tipped like a dog's to the breeze and his mind clearly wandering, he growled to catch the urban cat's attention and asked archly, 'Smell something, cat?'

The chill breeze groomed Kian's coat, stroking the satin blackness and white. He glanced contritely at the feral. 'Sorry, Shyler. The thing is, I'm a bit worried about those kittens. They'll be frightened, you see, if they can't find me.'

The tom stared at him as he might stare at a morsel that both tempted and repelled him. Finally he said, 'You're a sorry excuse for a cat, you are.'

Kian did not disagree: he turned his ears and strained to hear, in the dark of departing night he struggled to see, scanning in all directions for sign of the lost kittens, carelessly aware that he was, in the end, a sorry excuse for a cat.

The Shimmering Web

THE RAT PACED rapidly along the body of a felled swamp gum, avoiding the places where rot and termites and the tunnelling of grubs had weakened the wood to the point where collapse threatened even under the insignificant weight of a being such as itself. It reached the raggedy terminus of the trunk and lowered itself over the edge, its tail and rump anchoring it to the tree as its body stretched slinkily and its dainty paws grappled for the ground. The rat had an inborn aversion to the muzzy interval between night and day: it was such a brief interlude, the most delicate fragment of each day, but the rat knew it to be by far the most dangerous too. The rodent was an uninvited immigrant to the forest – its species had stepped over the bracken boundary generations earlier, attracted by the sapien rubbish that was dumped on the scrubby fringe, encouraged by the discovery that the natives were slow-witted and it was too easy to steal eggs and nestlings, to raid unguarded burrows for mouthfuls of flesh and bone – but it had been tracked here by its ancient enemy, the adaptable vagabond. This ghostly junction between night and day, a lifeless halt in the living flow of time, this was always the terrible time, when the enemy's eyes saw most true. The rat dropped from the trunk and dashed across the mud, stopping suddenly to taste the air, and all the motion that had been in its body was compressed into its head, into the grinding jaw and bobbing chin and short vibrating whiskers. Its eyes, dark as tar, did not blink, as if blinking might blind it at some crucial instant. Its scabrous tail flicked; it rubbed its pointed face with its paws and scampered boldly on. This was a big rat, one living through its prime: aware that it was exposed to peril it nonetheless moved with confidence, running low and spry, tacking briskly but not frantically along its path as though some undeniable force reeled it in. The rat was, in fact, following a route it had traversed nearly every night of its life: the course was signposted with the rodent's odour but the rat was utterly familiar with every speck of the trail and could have run its length without the aid of sight, sound or smell. The frequent halts to scrutinise its surrounds seemed to bore some inner part of itself that was no longer prey to instinctual concerns and met them only under sufferance. On it jogged, a creature the exact colour of the atmosphere around it, a sour yellow-white overlaid by a sheenless grey, no visible hint of its passing left on the trail that would soon lead it home. It stopped, as if slamming into stone, and propped on its hindquarters while its chary eyes scoured the underbrush, blood beating at its ribs. The forest air was thick with the coming winter, already frigid enough to sear the rat's warm lungs.

The cat's face was masked by the crimped, brilliantly green arm of a tree-fern; its eyes may never have been any colour but the fathomless black they became as they seized every trace of light and used it to pin the rat to the forest floor. The rat froze at the sight of the feline, saw itself become in the carnivore's mind something doomed, something dead, something consumed. Its head jerked, the plantlife blurring from its vision, the outline of the cat remaining focused and pristine. The cat's chin was close to the ground, one deceptively soft paw lifted as if too prim to put down. The ancient enemies stared at one another and it was the ancient stare, the stare that an aeon has never varied, as two enduring antagonists confronted each other for the first and last, fleeting and eternal, shrieking and silent, carmine-red and death-black instant. The cat, all power, met the rat, all intellect.

The rat spun: it lunged from the path and into the brush, a whistle of panic trilling from its gullet. Shyler plunged after it, noiseless as a shade. The scrub which gave the rodent imperfect cover hampered the cat's pursuit but both animals knew the chase would be over in a scatter of heartbeats. Shyler knew the rat was making for some nook of safety and that he had just moments in which to make the catch and kill; the rat knew it would die if it did not, in these same fevered moments, achieve its sanctuary. It raced, tail lifted to avoid the cat's crippling paws, the bracken stiff with frost and cutting at its head. Behind it, the cat swooped like a raven. Together, locked in fatal conflict, they made no sound at all. The rat ran like quicksilver and the cat came after it with diving, massive strides. Shyler could see the muscled place behind the rodent's ears where his teeth would sink with certainty, sublime.

And then, incredibly, the rat launched itself into the air: it astonished its pursuer by leaping, springy as a hare. Shyler, travelling with speed, could not stop himself immediately and even as misgiving flooded him he was carried helplessly forward. His blackened eyes still locked on the rat, he only felt the steel gridding that was suddenly under his feet; he saw the rat skim over a grille of crosshatched wire which had inexplicably formed a roof above his head. A cat is quick – the feral realised at once what was happening – but not always quick enough: even as Shyler wheeled, raging and dismayed, the door of the trap was triggered, smacking down across his tail but locking well enough to turn the open-ended trap into a hardy sealed cell that the feral smashed against, screaming. The slice of meat which lay stickily on the trip-plate was tossed up and trampled as the cat crashed around the cage. His snagged tail yanked him from his feet as he rushed the gridded walls; the air churned with a blizzard of hair and the mesh was sprayed with blood. He slammed his body from side to side, a whirlwind of wrath and terror, and the trap clanged and boomed. As he fought, a roar came from him which was the sound of every cat that's ever lived, every cougar, lynx and cheetah, every tiger, lion, jaguar and panther, every housecat that is fed and tended, every other that is discarded. The roar stilled the pulse of countless small beings of prey and it was heard by Cally and Marlo who were trekking dolefully along the roadside, it was heard by Jem, who lifted his chin from a leaf which cupped a sip of dew and licked his lips, thinking, and then began to run.

Kian, too, ran: he was nearby, stalking a crackle in the scrub, and he was guided to the feral by the clashing of the cage as much as by the incarcerated animal's reverberating bellow. A cat has no instinct for aiding another and it was curiosity that made Kian seek out the feral, a need to know what dreadful thing could so panic the tom and, knowing it, be better able to avoid it himself. He moved with caution through the damp underwood, afraid that whatever tortured Shyler would make a slashing grab for him; when he could smell but not see the feral and the clashing noise was loudest he slunk to his belly and crept over the ground. He craned his head round the trunk of a tree-fern, tasting air in the pit of his throat. What he saw seemed to jolt electricity through him, sparking every hair. Beyond the fern was a cleared circle of earth and in the middle of the circle Shyler was enclosed in a large, boxlike, wire-grid cage. The walls of the cage spangled silver with dew and Kian finally realised what the ferals had meant, when they spoke of steely cobwebs.

The urban cat had never seen an animal trap before, but he understood some of what he saw. Kian had been shut inside a box himself, and he knew the peril behind lids and encasing walls. He hunkered to the ground, aware he should disappear, unsure where to go. Under the skewing influence of Shyler's rage he found it difficult to order his thoughts. The feral had incited himself into frenzy, spitting and twisting and thrashing, assailing the unfeeling wire. His scrabbling claws had stripped his skin so blood and fur occupied the trap with him, as if he had not been caught alone. The end of his tail, pinioned by the door, lay lank as something amputated. Kian crouched, confused and mute in the face of such hysteria, and long moments passed lethargically while the feral thundered in the cage and the urban cat contemplated his paws. Movement made him look up to see the dusky watcher of the forest sliding swiftly between the mountain ash, veering close and then away – Kian sensed its elation, and its tempering concern. Behind the rugged arm of a bird's-nest fern he glimpsed the masks of Cally and Marlo; forgetting to be surprised or pleased he simply gazed at them as he would at a flavourless beetle. Cally was staring at him as if expecting some final decision: when she realised he had nothing to say she hissed, 'Kian? What shall we do?'

Marlo's eyes were on the flailing tom, whose fight was beginning to fade, now, whose protests were becoming less shrill. 'We should leave,' he announced blankly. 'It's bad luck for Shyler. Come on, let's go.'

But the three cats stayed where they were, hidden in the powdery dawn, separated from each other by the circle of tramped earth and the rectangular skeleton of the cage, which listed but did not topple as Shyler battered his head on its roof. Kian continued to stare at the scene, at the lifeless tip of the feral's tail, at the glimmering contrivance that made up the trap's locking device. He mulled over this fastening, his mind shallow as a rainpool. Distantly it occurred to him that he'd seen similar devices in the past, comparable arrangements of hooks and rods and springs. Contraptions not greatly unlike this lock had been attached to cupboards and doors in the house he had shared with Ellen. Kian had devoted entire nights to fathoming the trickery behind them and the rewards for doing so had flowed as they should. He had taught himself to pull window latches and grant his own freedom; he had outfoxed the jamb that held shut the door which would have stood, otherwise, between him and his box of food. Within his cloudy mind a thought came to Kian, brilliant as the spark off striking stones. He remembered, as he cowered in the scrub and the wild dawn rose around him, that he was a domestic cat, a born manipulator.

Cats are logical: reflex rules the feline, but what a cat

doesn't do instinctively is often done after scrupulous planning and consideration. The ability to think rationally is a trait that has its advantages and over generations the cat has nurtured the pondering tendency in itself. As a result, cats have not only excellent powers of deduction but also the capacity to remember what they manage to teach themselves. All cats, therefore, are clever – but only the cat who has lived in a house has had reason to turn his cleverness to the outsmarting of sapien-made locks.

Kian got to his feet, brushing past the fronds and stepping into the clearing. He approached the trap with sober care, smelling more distinctly the muggy reek of the bait, seeing flecks of it dotted in Shyler's shabby coat. The slate tom was snorting, heaving air through a bleeding nose, breathing it out as a tuneless yowl. He lay still with exhaustion but as Kian approached he staggered up, wanting to run. The pull on his tail made him drop bonelessly and he sagged, gasping, on his side. Frightened and distrustful he growled at Kian, his eyes green as peridot, the pupils needle-thin. Kian ignored the perilous look: he sniffed the cage and ran his gaze along the wand of metal that was the mainstay of the lock. There was, as he'd expected, nothing alive about the cage – it in itself could do no cat any harm. He raised a paw and touched the blunt-nosed wand, feeling its coldness through the flesh of his pads. The rigid wire meshing formed neat square holes and Kian slipped a paw through one of them and wagged it investigatively. Shyler's eyes flamed and he swiped at the snowy foot: 'Get lost!' he spluttered. 'Get – get away!'

Kian judiciously withdrew the paw. 'What happened, cat?'

Shyler showed his teeth, pink from bitten lips. One ear twitched with fear and pain. 'That rattus, he's a wily bastard, didn't I tell you?'

'Rat.' Kian's tail shivered. 'When you get out, kill him.'

The feral said nothing; his head sank to rest on the wire, his eyes drooped closed. 'Kian,' Marlo muttered, 'we better leave. The cobweb wants every cat.'

Kian looked around at the tabby, who stood tensely on the edge of the circle. He saw that Jem had tracked the feral's distress and stood, now, in a channel dug by the runoff of rain, invisible but for a golden glint of the eyes. His lost kittens were found, and Kian knew Marlo was right. The trap was not a living thing, yet everything about it – the barren arena it stood in, the trees above it, the stamped earth below – stank with menace. Cally skittered from behind the bird's-nest, stopping at the tabby's side. 'Please, Kian,' she whispered, 'let's go.'

Kian looked back at the trap. He stared at the metal bar. He remembered that, at home in the house with Ellen, he had been a masterful magician, a flicker-of-catches and springer-of-doors, and plundering the food cupboard had been the least of his tricks. He had taught himself to shake the garden gate until the hasp jumped and the gate fell away, allowing him to stroll on; he had seen that the fridge was equally vulnerable and could wrench the slabbed door open and keep it open too, while he raided, with an astutely placed hind foot. He had learned that if he rubbed his flank against the sliding flyscreen he could shunt the screen aside, letting in both insects and himself. He had known how to use his weight to swing a door-handle down; he had even, on several occasions, performed the difficult manoeuvre of grasping the knob of Ellen's bedroom door and rotating it enough to free the bolt and gain access to the bed. Tilting handles, dangling hasps, pendulous chains, heavy bolts, an array of fastenings of every size and design: these things were, to such a magician, as trifling as toys. Kian hedged closer to the trap, his steps soundless on the dirt. He stared at the lock, grazing it with his sensitive whiskers. He saw how a slim rod, sliding vertically, had passed through a metal loop and how its tip sat just above a small cap, also metal, which would fit the rod as a shell fits a snail. The bar was striving to slot into this cap, emitting tinks of frustration. Its intentions were being spoiled, Kian saw, because Shyler's tail was caught in the door: a delicate balance had been upset and now the lock could only imperfectly close. 'Shyler,' he murmured, as if volume would ruin everything, 'stay still. Stay perfectly still, all right?'

The feral didn't answer, the breath whistling in his nose. Dawn was suffused with an aquamarine-blue, icing the canopy with light; across the forest's floor a numbing breeze razored, gusting ahead of it a graveyard of dry leaves. Kian explored the lock with his whiskers, straining his wits to decipher its mystery. It seemed to him that the trap's door was held shut by a single snagging, the junction between the rod and the metal loop. Kian tested this steely crossroad, biting it gently, pressing it with a paw. The pressure tightened the door on Shyler's tail, and the stricken feral yowled.

'Kian?'

Kian did not look around; his eyes tracked the rigging of shafts and springs. There was no reason why he could not defeat this thing, he who had defeated many others.

'Kian . . .'

He levelled his sights on it, trying to think. Success lay in thinking things out: to begin, all he needed was a moment of bright clarity.

'Kian –'

'*Shut up!*' The black-and-white cat wheeled on Marlo, who hissed venomously in return. The tabby was not so easily intimidated as he had once been.

'Squirt on you!' the striped tom spat. 'You want to get caught too? You want us all to get caught?'

'Shut it, I told you!'

'Shut it yourself, Kian! It's not safe here, can't you see? Forget Shyler, there's nothing you can do!'

Kian, infuriated, rushed at the tabby, who scuttled behind the buffer of tree-fern, hackles up and glaring. 'Have it your way!' he yelped. 'Get caught, if you want to – disappear, for all I care! I'm leaving: Jem, Cally, you should leave too!'

With that he spun and ran, swiftly vanishing in the smir. The kittens, camouflaged in leaves, looked to Kian desperately. 'Stay where you are!' he told them, and they obeyed, though it took every scrap of willpower, and Jem grizzled miserably. Kian turned to the caged feral, who drawled, 'That mewler is right. You should go.'

Kian was terse. 'Listen to me, Shyler. Have you ever heard of a cat escaping a cobweb?'

The feral gurgled, sluggishly amused. 'I've heard that some have done it, but I never met a cat that did.'

'What will happen, if you don't get out of the cage?'

Shyler shifted on the hard grille. 'The cage will disappear. It won't be here when the sun falls. When it goes, I'll go with it. I don't know where to, but I won't be coming back.' The tom blinked dully. 'It doesn't matter, Kian. It's the way things are.'

Kian's tail flickered. 'In your world, maybe. Not in mine.'

He fixed his attention on the trap, on its body of mesh and wire. He noted the loops and hooks and chains, he saw that the cage itself was pegged loosely to the ground. He saw how the door of the trap was hinged from the top, making it shut down but open up. His gaze traversed the cold structure, his ears listened for its secrets. Tell me, he asked it: show me. He focused on the contraption with the terrible feline intensity that can slow the beating of a heart, an unearthly raylike concentration that skewers and disables. The forest drained out of Kian's awareness, the wind ceased to blow. The kittens had never been, and the grief their existence caused him was soothed away. He was a proud cat on his own turf, intelligent, well-fed, warmed at the fireside. There was nothing urgent or vital about the problem before him. He was a contented cat considering a puzzle: how would he solve it, in the peaceful security of his home? How would he, at home, bend this lock to his will?

If he was home and life was good and it didn't really matter whether he conquered this lock or not, if he were home, fed and complacent and free of the worries that had lately been heaped upon him, he would have the patience to realise that the metal rod and the metal loop must be disentangled. He recalled hasps on gates, latches on doors. This was no different, and no more difficult. The rod moved when he nudged it – it moved up. When he took his paw from it, it slipped down. It endeavoured to slot, irretrievably, into the metal cap. Only the slight bulk of Shyler's tail stopped it doing so.

'Kian.'

The urban cat glanced past the wire. Shyler was sitting up. His coat was wet and matted with dirt. 'Don't move,' Kian said gruffly, careless what the feral had to say. At home, unravelling the enigma of a lock, the only other thought he allowed himself was a vague anticipation of what success would mean. Success was breaking in when he was out, it was helping himself to the contents of the pantry or bundling up to sleep on Ellen's bed. Cats are imaginative: Kian, so homesick, had no difficulty pretending that, if he could unpick the lock before him, he would swing aside a door to his own, distant world.

'Kian . . .'

The pupils of Kian's eyes, in the spreading light, had contracted to expose the lime-green of each iris. He touched the rod with a claw. The device was essentially simple – he understood it now. The metal wand moved smoothly under the influence of his paw. He could push the bar up, through the shining loop. When he had done so, the cage's door would be held shut by nothing more than its own insignificant weight.

Kian concentrated as if he had, in his sights, a dazzling, dancing, destroyable bird. With the flat of a paw he forced the bar up. It slid cleanly through the loop. The trap was open. Kian dropped his foot, delighted, and the rod plunged down, through the loop, halting a fraction above the cap. Foiled and cursing inwardly, Kian, catlike, gave no sign of emotion. Thinking quickly, he sprang to the roof of the cage, startling the captive Shyler and flustering the kittens, who tensed, ready to flee. Kian, his feet splaying on the grid, peered through the mesh at the tom. 'Listen, cat,' he said. 'The bar falls down, so I have to lift it up. When I do, lean against the door and you'll get out. All right?'

Shyler only gaped at him and Kian saw that the tom made no sense of the instructions, that the language of mechanisms was utterly foreign to the wild cat. It was, Kian thought, an unfortunate moment in which to score a victory over the supercilious ferals. He lowered a paw past the edge of the cage and grappled for the bar. The dewy metal was difficult to grip and he hissed as the rod slithered through his claws.

'Kian!' This was Marlo, cantering unexpectedly from the scrub. He stood on his toes, looking back the way he had come. 'There's a noise. Something's wrong.'

Kian swatted the bar, his foot glancing off it. The trap rocked under him and Shyler stumbled against a wall. A distant stirring in the forest made Marlo scamper sideways, his ears bent to his skull. He had not returned in the hope of warning his companions about the approaching danger – rather, his safest retreat had lain in retracing his steps – and his animal heart banged painfully as he lingered in the clearing. He whirled, black-eyed, toward Kian and the cage. 'Can't you hear it?'

Kian could hear it, a crisp rustling passed from tree to tree, the sigh of spongy earth beneath stolid weight. He hung over the cage, hectically studying the lock. A bushlark startled and flew off crying, and Shyler looked up at Kian. 'Get lost, cat,' he breathed.

'I've nearly got it . . .'

'Kian,' Jem piped, 'it's coming closer! We have to run!'

'Kian.' Cally scurried from the bracken. 'It's a man.'

Marlo jumped the ferns and was gone. The kittens

shrank to the brink of the clearing, snarling at the trees. Shyler, in the cage, moaned with fear; the forest's fleet shadow winged into the canopy. Kian felt urgently for the bar, his paw smacking the grille. He heard the break of tiny twigs, the whish of bark pulled over the ground, he recognised the sloping gait of a human on the move. His whiskers felt the sweep of air as the kittens turned and ran. The metal jinked as his paw clamped the bar and, pinched by a peculiar pain, he hoisted the rod as high as it would go. 'Now, Shyler!' he gasped. 'Run – run!'

Shyler understood that, and obeyed. He threw himself against the door. The force of his lunge jerked the bar from Kian's grip and almost threw him from the cage. Shyler slammed head-first into the grid and crumpled, stunned. The door of the trap had held: Kian chirped, incredulous. He scanned the lock frantically and only as the man pushed past the fern and stepped into the clearing did the urban cat realise that the cage door was fastened by not one bar, but two. Another rod lay on the opposite side of the door, a perfect reflection of the first but for the fact that this one was lodged resolutely within its metal shell.

For Kian, everything slowed. Eternities passed before he hauled his sights from the second bar and looked at the man. The man was slight and smelt sweetly of rot, the smell of the forest floor; his clothes were the olive shade of eucalypt leaves, as if he lived in trees. His face was ageless, smooth as river stone; his hair brushed his head like feathers and his hands hung slack and empty, curving at his sides. What he saw in the clearing made him stop, riveted, and the cat on the roof of the cage stared silently back at him.

The urban cat was aware that the feral, penned below him, was spitting like a bushfire at the ranger, demonically raging and afraid. Kian, however, felt no fear, not a sliver. He had been acquainted with humans all his life – he had been held in human hands when still wet from being born. He was familiar with human frailties: he knew his claws drew blood from them, that he could outrun them, that his body could be like liquid or sand in their arms. The ranger must have expected him to flee – surely every able cat in the forest flew from him – but Kian was not in the habit of running from humans. He stared at the man, and the man stared at him. The ebony hair along Kian's spine lifted; he folded his ears, exposed his teeth and snarled murderously. He told the man that he would, without question, attack if he had to: if the man came any closer, he would be *shredded*. And the man stayed where he was, making no move: the man understood.

A tame cat, accustomed to the sight and scent of humans, moving with the slowest motion and keeping his sights on the one transfixed before him, Kian reached down and caught the metal wand. He had no real reason for doing so – he had already seen that lifting the bar did not grant Shyler his freedom. But, through the commotion in his mind, Kian was remembering his home, his grassy garden, his favourite places in the sun. He was remembering Ellen, the old woman who did not breathe any more. He remembered the warm taste of a pigeon squab and Ellen asking him to set the downy creature free. She was making the no noise, no no no. Instead he'd romped away with the fledgling between his jaws, a gleeful and ungovernable beast of a cat. An ungovernable, defiant cat, who taught himself to stalk a sparrow without ringing his collar's bell; an ungovernable, defiant, lawless cat, who would pick a lock simply because he resented its presence in his world. He was a cat who, driven far from his territory, would turn around smartly and walk straight home; an audacious and independent cat, who did whatever he pleased. And what pleased him now was to show this man that he was not afraid, that he was no cat to be trifled with, that he would not do anything expected of him. His rebellious glare impaling the ranger, he caught the rod and pulled the bar up, beyond the metal looping. It charmed him to see astonishment transfuse the man's face and for the briefest moment Kian softened, repented, forgiving all. He became, for that instant, a tame cat again, and felt an urge to let this human stroke him, to lift his chin and close his eyes and allow himself to be scratched. He pulled the bar up and he held it, remembering his sundered life.

Shyler, jailed below him, rammed the trap's door with such primitive strength that the second rod flexed like a reed: the door twisting outwards, the scurfy tom shot through the gap like a zephyr. Kian, taken by surprise, sprang into the air screaming; he hit the ground at a gallop and sprinted after the feral and his last glimpse of the clearing was silver, like the trap, olive, like the ranger, blue with the dawn, grey with animal hair. There was whiteness, too, in the man's hovering face, bloodless with bewilderment, pinkened with wonder.

Kian rushed through the understorey, swift and supple as the wind. He knew that Shyler raced just ahead of him, that the kittens and Marlo dashed somewhere alongside. He heard the Earth's call in his paws and it was clearer than it had ever been, grew louder and more triumphant as he increased his valiant speed. He soared over rocks and scrummy bracken, the orange light of morning pouring in his eyes. Leaves and pebbles tumbled in his wake, spindly fingers of scrub pulled scraps of hair from him, making a trail that glistened and shone. Together the cats left the trap and the ranger far behind and when they reached a place that was overgrown and secure Kian threw himself on his back in the dirt and Jem and Cally dived on him like pitching seabirds, punching the air from his lungs, overjoyed to be with him again.

Grassland

THE FIVE CATS had arrived at the outskirts of the forest. It was morning and they lay quietly, each some distance from the others but bonded by stillness and tranquillity. This fringe of the forest had caught fire in the past and the trunks of grey gums and peppermints bore charred scars; the flames had encouraged young eucalypts to shoot toward the sun, and bottlebrush and wattle had rebounded leggily. Sprinkled in the scrub were random pieces of rubbish, plastic rings of beer-cans, the severed head of a child's doll, a lighter, a bent spoon. These baubles of sapien jetsam formed a piecemeal frontier between the forest that towered behind the cats and the grass-land that spread in front – there was no fenced boundary or wall. The forest simply petered out: as the cats had journeyed on after escaping the trapped clearing they had seen the canopy thin until it was so tatty and full of holes that Jem was reminded of the lace he'd ripped, as a kitten, from the hem of Ellen's apron. And finally the forest had come to an end: the land that now spread before the animals was open and slanted and the wind brushed the grass tidy and mussed it messy again. A scattering of eucalypts also grew on this plain, late-comers to or outcasts from the forest, and Kian wondered if he must wait until concrete was below his feet before he could feel he'd left wilderness behind. Nestled in a desiccated bed of green fronds, he was purring softly to himself, the soil warm beneath his belly, his head rubbed by watery sunshine. There was no urgency to his hunger, and his coat was comfortably dry. The song of the Earth thrummed gently in his bones, companionable and trustworthy. Settling his chin on his paws Kian reflected that, although his stay in the forest had been horrendous in so many ways, there had also been occasions when he'd felt, as he felt now, a perfect, diamondlike sense of serenity.

The cats had left the steely cobweb far behind – an entire day and night had passed since Shyler broke out of the cage and the travellers had maintained a brisk pace for much of that time, stopping only to sleep in the drizzling afternoon and to hunt in the dripping dusk. As night had seeped into the sky, Cally, attracted by the ducklike quacking of frogs, discovered a pond full of the bite-sized amphibians, and the cats had chased the glistening acrobats as the moon darkened from gauzy to shell-white. It had been beside the pond that Shyler, nursing a bilious frog-filled stomach, finally recovered sufficient composure to speak about the trap. 'What did you do back there?' he'd asked Kian. 'How did you do it?'

Kian had flexed a dexterous paw. His one regret was that Janshar, that odious tom cat, had not been witness to the rescue. He knew that the tale of Shyler's escape would be told throughout the forest and perhaps crafted into legend, but that the retellings and his absence would soon combine to distort and doubtlessly diminish his own role in the drama. Cats have little respect for the truth, and the best Kian could hope was that his heroics in the clearing were not too rapidly poached by Shyler and Marlo and converted into heroics of their own. He had slapped his tail at the thought, more bemused than nettled: he would always remember these nights and days in the forest with the ferals, but the forest would quickly forget him, and to the wild cats he was just a passing oddity. It wouldn't be long before no trace of him remained anywhere in this place – but the forest would haunt him, Kian knew, forever.

So, while the kittens slept and bats swooped overhead, Kian had sat in the darkness explaining to Marlo and Shyler what the bars and loops on the trap had meant, and describing in detail the technique he had used to outwit the mechanism. He told them how the escape had depended on the fortuitous pinning of Shyler's tail, which had hindered the sliding of the bolt. He counselled them against pointless fury and panic, should a day come when they found themselves similarly caged. Thoughtful analysis and effort were the things to set a cat free. As he spoke, Kian hoped he was leaving these wild ones a gift of gratitude, something worthwhile they might remember of him, and the ferals had tried hard to concentrate on what he was saying, Marlo even ignoring the blind creep of a leech past his paw. Then had come the flutter of a grounded bird and both ferals had vanished in a blink. Kian sighed to see them go but he supposed the choice they made was right. The feral life was short and fast, it was kill and mate and fight and run. A trap was only one of untold hazards which could make a wild cat disappear and such perils, disheartening to think of, were less so when accepted with a nonchalant grace.

After dozing by the pond they had meandered into the night, drawing close and straying apart. Jem heard sounds that were familiar to him now, the scurrying and buzzing and creaking and groans. When the cut-throat screams of a territory brawl ricocheted off the trees the cats had paused to listen, interested, but not agitated or afraid. They knew things, now, that they had not known earlier in their journey, and one thing they'd learned was that not everything in the forest revolved around them. If they stayed hidden and made no noisy claim, whole dramas of life might boil around them but they would come through unscathed. In the deep of night they had seen the forest become luminous, as the canopy, growing skimpy, gave way to the light of the moon, and tracts of a lush star-studded sky unrolled between clusters of trees. Shyler had stopped, staring up at it. His ears pivoted and he looked at Kian. 'You sure this is the way?'

Pinpoints of light were mirrored in his eyes as Kian gazed at stars he'd feared he might never again see. 'Yes, I'm sure.'

'. . . The forest is finishing.'

'Yes, I think it is.'

The knowledge clearly bothered the grey tom, who glanced repeatedly and doubtfully at the sky. Kian remembered how the thought of the wild cats following him home had once obsessed and incensed him: how ludicrous that suspicion felt now. Janshar, who had seemed such a dangerous threat to Kian's range, had never been a danger at all: Kian only now understood that the ferals would never leave their wilderness. This was their home, just as the trim suburban streets belonged to him. Innately secretive creatures, the very sight of the fragmenting canopy made them feel exposed; he tried to picture Marlo napping on a doormat, and simply could not.

And then, near dawn, their journeying had brought them here, to the edge of the forest, where the scant canopy ceased to be any canopy at all and the raddled undergrowth gave way to this carpet of flourishing green: Kian knew that when the wan sun rose they would see nothing but white clouds above them and hear only the sweep of the sward below. The darkness of the forest lifted from him like a stone and he breathed in air that flowed in free currents, unhampered by the crowding of fern and trees. Kian looked back at the forest lovingly, now he'd reached its very edge, though within its black depths he had found little to like. His journey was going to take him much further, but he felt a great sense of achievement to have already come this far. The kittens were tired, and in the hushness of night's end Kian had let them rest; they twined their lean bodies in the warmth of one another and were instantly asleep. He wondered what was waiting for them at the end of their long walk home, when they'd crossed this field and maybe many more, after they'd wandered for days along footpaths and roads . . . not Ellen, but maybe the man. Kian would need to watch them, and speedily teach them every trick he knew, because life, at home, might not always be easy – yet surely any life would be better than the brief, uncivilised existence that was all the forest offered them.

Marlo and Shyler stretched out in the litter and Kian settled amid the moss and fronds, away from the swirling breeze. It was pleasant to lie there, in company with the ferals, watching bat silhouettes flap noiselessly across the charcoal sky. Night still cloaked the forest but the sun hovered somewhere just beneath the horizon and Kian felt trembly in anticipation of its rays. After days below the canopy, it felt like an age since he'd seen a sunrise. A birdwing of blackness moved in the leaves and he looked up at the last trees to see the forest's shadow skulking in the branches, his own spectral escort to the limit of the wilderness. This forest, Kian knew, despised and dreaded cats, as it rightly dreaded all alien creatures; the forest was harmed and changed by cats, yet would not inflict harm in return. A living thing made of living things, the forest was an essence of Life, and its nature was to shelter and preserve – to protect even those creatures that would rip it, eventually, apart. Kian, surrounded by sapien castoffs, told the dark spirit that he, at least, was leaving, never to return: I won't trouble you, he promised, any more.

'You shouldn't travel when it's light.' The urban cat looked at Shyler, who spoke without shifting his gaze from the field. 'Not out there,' said the feral. 'You should wait till it's night again.'

The grey tom would stop breathing before he'd admit the open grassland disconcerted him, and Kian was touched by his awkward concern. 'We'll be all right,' he said. 'I don't want to waste a day sitting here.'

'Where's your territory, anyway?' Marlo turned argent eyes to him. 'Can you see it from here?'

'Oh, no. We've got a long way to travel yet – the forest was only the beginning. My home feels nearer than it was, but it still feels very far away. When I find streets and roads, then I'll be getting closer. When everywhere I look there are streets and cars and houses, and lawns and rooftops and roads, dogs on leads, birds behind wire – that's when I'll almost be there. These trees and ferns and creeks and things – there's none of this wildness at home.'

Cally's voice startled the cats, for they had not noticed the kittens wake. The young cats lay side by side, coats fluffing with the breeze. 'I'll miss the forest, though,' said the calico cub. 'I like it here.'

'And me,' Jem added. 'I like it too.'

Kian glanced approvingly at the siblings and Cally saw that he thought they were only being polite to the ferals – it would not occur to him, she realised, to think a cat might prefer the precarious life. She would never leave Kian, and she would not resent a moment of following him, but when she slept she would dream of the forest, Cally knew, until the last of her days.

The sun had finally crept over the skyline, a pearl of wintry brilliance swaddled in boggy cloud. Kian, as if called, made to stand – and sank in the ferns again. He wached the morning touch the faces of his companions, thinning their pupils with its soft light. All over his body Marlo carried the evidence of his clash with the possum; movement seemed painful for him, one ear was crusted stiff as wood. One of Kian's own ears had been nicked during the encounter with the dog and its peak would carry a permanent split; his nose had been sliced first by Whit and then by Janshar, and his skirmish with the red tom had left him sprinkled with flesh wounds. Shyler, never neat, had been made preposterously bedraggled by his frenzy inside the animal cage: escaping had stripped sheets of hair from him, and the end of his tail was noticeably bent. Only the kittens, lithe Jem and Cally, had come through the forest more or less unscathed.

Kian stood again, more sure of himself this time. A sense of excitement bloomed in him and he was suddenly eager to get going, to trot out boldly to meet whatever was waiting for him. He wanted to run – to gallop the entire distance home – because he did not think he had a dot of patience left for walking or resting. Cats are never mawkish, and it pleased him to know that farewells would not greatly delay his departure. The kittens were on their feet and watching him. Marlo and Shyler sat up but did not step forward, loath to leave the last shade of the forest. 'Are you sure you won't come a little further?' Kian asked them nevertheless. 'You might find something to eat in the field.'

'There's rabbits out there,' remarked Marlo. 'I can smell them.'

'Yeah.' Shyler flicked his tail. 'Grab a little one if you can, Kian.'

Kian's gaze scanned the grimy masks of the ferals. Behind them the forest soared, great ramshackle trunks of ash and stringybark linking waxen sky to fertile soil, the underwood thick with gorse and miry fern. Somewhere in its depths was the water clowder and the she-cat Tey; somewhere in there was Janshar, strutting with false glory, and Fyfe, the genial fox. In there were wagtails and earthworms and possums and mice, bandicoots and black snakes stretched out on lukewarm stones. In there existed a complete and self-sufficient world which had no use at all for buildings or fences or collars or roads. Kian longed to leave it, but hesitated. 'What will you do now?' he asked Shyler. 'Where will you go?'

The smoky tom twinged his whiskers. 'You know me, Kian. I go where the whim takes me.'

'Oh, yes, I remember. The whip-poor-will. I'll think of you in every breeze.' He looked to the tabby. 'What about you, Marlo?'

The young feral lifted his chin. 'I want a range. I'm not going back to the clowder, no way. I killed the possum. I went back to warn you about the ranger. I might fight Janshar, and take that territory. I deserve it more than he does.'

Kian's lips curved. 'Yes, I think you do.'

'. . . I'll make a better warrior than him.'

'Yes,' agreed the suburban cat, 'you will.'

Shyler and Marlo watched the three refugees turn and set off through the grass, the blades dragging over Cally's ears and showering her with dew. Marlo glanced at Shyler but the tom seemed drowsy and in no hurry to leave, so the tabby settled down on his paws. The ferals watched the urban cats slip across the paddock until the dip of the land shouldered them from view; then the tabby looked again at the bigger cat, who flared his whiskers and said, 'Let's go.'

The paddock quickly proved unpleasant walking: the grass was drenched and the coats of Kian and the kittens were soon cloyed with water, their bellies dripping, their legs leaden, their noses wet and raw. The grass formed lumpen tussocks and the cats slid and slithered over them. Mats of grass concealed swampy puddles, pungent and quaggy with decay. The wind, chill but bisected in the forest, blew unchecked and frigid over the land and the cats folded their ears, hopelessly trying to keep its icy claws from them. Kian stopped walking when he saw that Cally lagged and he watched her make her way laboriously to him, her head lowered against the gale so she did not see a puddle before tripping into it and being splashed to the chin. Jem had halted beside Kian and stood despondent, shaking first one leg and then another. Dewdrops festooned his flanks and he had a small mushy leaf on his ear. The grass whispered to itself continuously, a sly demonish mutter relayed by the wind. Kian looked behind him, to the forest: the slope of the land had blocked the underbrush from view but he could still see gangling limbs of the trees. A shiver ran through him and he sank to his haunches. In front of him the grassland continued forever, the shifty green rolling to the horizon, meeting a washed-out sky. He knew the marsh would end somewhere, but if they must toil through every stride of it as they were doing, they would be exhausted and possibly drowned before the sun reached its summit. And yet, it was absolutely necessary to cross this field: despite the rock-hard tussocks and the heaviness of his legs Kian could hear it clearly, the Earth's magnetic, beating song.

And then, standing high on his haunches, he saw it: a path. There was a path wending through the paddock and he felt the sense of friendly recognition he'd had, in the forest, each time he had encountered the road. The path was a serpentine track in the dirt, and the grass, beside this trail, grew less energetically than it did elsewhere, as if regularly pressed under hooves or wheels. Kian bounced across the field like a hare, landing after several leaps in the gummy brown trough of the path. He could smell, embedded in its surface, the distinct odour of petrol, and saw the cylinder of a cigarette butt. 'This is better,' he said to Jem and Cally, who had scrambled after him and stood, braced with cold. 'This is better, isn't it?'

And it was better: the wind howled like a revenant, bleaker and stronger than ever, but the walking-track made easier travelling and the cats were able to trot despite the gale, leaving behind them flowerlike pawprints which were preserved a moment in moisture before melting into the ground. From the broad-backed tussocks burst starlings and blackbirds who flopped about in the breeze and ahead of them Kian saw two velvety ravens scoop the air and fly away across the paddock, cawing throatily. For a happy instant he believed they were flying from him, the baneful predator, but then he heard the rumble of human voices and realised he wasn't the only intimidating creature in the field. Indeed, the kittens were reacting with terror to the sound, whirling to face it with hair spiked the length of their spines. They stumbled back from the sight of the sapiens, eyes blackened, ears flat, their mouths slung and hissing.

Kian, however, did not move. The humans – two males, with a scalded, sulphurous smell to them – were some distance away, although they were strolling in the direction of the cats. It seemed to Kian that there was no reason to run: running was the reaction of a wild cat, a frightened cat, a cat who had no need for the humans' respect, but Kian was not wild, and he would not let the kittens be wild. Soon he would bring them home, and the siblings' lives would be misery if they learned the wild cat's fear. He stood brazenly in the middle of the path and watched the men dawdle closer, knowing he would dart away the instant they took a step too near but wanting, too, to let them see him, to realise he was not feral, to understand he'd lived his life alongside their world – to know also that he was a defiant cat, courageous and unafraid. The worrying thought crossed his mind that one of them might be the ranger, tracking him like a hound, but the ranger had blended into the surrounds, and these men were stark against it. The ranger had smelt of earth and leaves, as if he'd been born in the crook of a tree, but the breeze blowing past the two men brought to Kian the odour of grease. The kittens cowering behind him, Kian watched the pair ramble to a halt: one raised an arm in the direction of the gliding birds, and the other lifted a dark stick – a stick, Kian saw, that must not be a stick, for it uttered a boom of noise. The noise struck a raven and the bird somersaulted, its great wings spread wide. It made no sound as it fell and when it dropped into the grass only feathers stayed to mark where it had been, and these were snatched away by the gale. The man lowered the stick to his side and barked sounds into the breeze; the other man, shorter and paler, turned his head and looked at Kian. He took the stick in his own hands and brought it to his chin. Kian heard a blackbird cry as it sheared past on the wind. Only then did he see clearly the mistakes he had made. 'Run,' he told the kittens, '*run* –'

There was a whiplash of noise, as if the atmosphere was bursting, and the bullet tore through the grass to the side of the black-and-white cat, who spun on his claws and ran. The kittens sprinted away from the track and as he glimpsed them diving through the grass Kian recalled how camouflaged they were, Cally so mottled, Jem so pitch, so unlike his shiny self. 'Run!' he shouted to them, and part of him was abashed to hear it, such a stupid, unnecessary thing to say. 'Don't stop running!'

The air boomed again, a sound like a landslide, and Kian, running, fell in the grass and was on his feet immediately, hot and cold everywhere. There was a lonely peppercorn standing in the paddock and he swung toward it, stumbling on his sodden paws, his heart rampaging at his ribs. Mucky water plashed in his eyes and into his open mouth. He raced, the frozen air searing his throat, his white feet flying across the grass, spattering flecks of mud. A cat is fast, but never as fast as it wants to be, and it seemed to Kian that despite his agonising efforts the peppercorn was coming no closer – then its hanging branches threw their shade over him and leaves swept his soiled face. The base of the tree was jungled with weeds and Kian dug in amongst them, spiderwebs netting his muzzle and legs, the vegetation a raspy cushion beneath him so he could not feel the ground. He wriggled about, huddling down, peeping back the way he had come. Through the tangles he saw the men stopped where the cats had stood on the path, the shorter of them squatting to examine the earth, the stick balanced over a shoulder. They scanned the paddock and Kian knew they were searching for him and for the kittens, and pressed deeper into the weeds. He could not see the cubs anywhere and trusted that to the men they were equally invisible. He looked at his wound and it was only now beginning to pour and it relieved him to know he hadn't left behind a scarlet trail that would lead to his hiding-place in the blades. He did not think he could keep running; he was unutterably tired and needed to rest. He laid his head on the ethereal weeds and closed his stinging eyes. His heart was beating fraughtly and he willed it some peace and even as he did so he felt it beginning to slow. He felt warm, the warmth of a fireside, and he wondered if the sun had sought him through the grass and fanned its rays for him. He was drifting toward home when his foreleg jerked and roused him, dazed; he opened his eyes and stared wearily at the blood that had saturated his side and was trickling in streams, now, through the bedding of weeds.

A cat, sometimes, knows better than to fight. Kian shut his eyes and allowed himself to sink. The alcove was snug and concealing, and he sensed he was safe. He was aware of the spicy fragrance of the grassland and of the sturdy trunk at his back. He heard the melancholy whistle of the wind planing the field but the thick weeds shielded him from the blustering cold, and the peppercorn's branches cascaded a veil over the morning's glare. He thought distantly of kittens, and remembered he'd once been young himself; a strong recollection of wildness went through him, and a puzzling need to be somewhere. He thought of the sun, of water, of earth and air, he remembered how it felt to hone his claws on the hard bark of a quince tree. The blood falling from him was warm as a hand run down his body. He thought he had something important to do but did not quite know what it was, nor his reasons for wanting to do it. Later he heard a bird chime, and another answer its cry: the birds told him that the men were gone, but Kian didn't open his eyes. He heard the breeze drop and calm drape over the paddock, the whining and whispering stilled. There came a tiny tremor that must have been an insect, for it cruised near and reeled away. He was not cold, but he curled his body tighter.

It occurred to Kian that it was tiring, to breathe. The weeds fluttered on his final breath and it was a relief to be freed from the lifetime burden of filling his lungs again. The melody of the Earth was a hymn in his feet and he realised, with startled joy, that everything around him was home.

It was a dragonfly that swooped Kian, the last dragonfly of the season. As soon as the gale weakened it had taken to the air, its crucifix frame spindle-thin, its blunt wings spangling a rainbow of colour. It had fulfilled all the small requirements of its existence and its flying had a lax purposelessness – it flew, now, simply because it could. It sailed past Jem, who had crawled from a waterlogged thicket and whose golden gaze skimmed the paddock. The sunlight, loosed from the turbulent grip of the wind, capped his head warmly. His jet nose found Kian and he trembled with strange aversion. Marooned alone in the billowing expanse of the field, the black kitten stumbled about in circles, mewing pitifully. He wanted, and did not want, to call for Kian. He looked at the sky and at the stern monarchal trees and saw how insignificant he was, how tiny and inconsequential in the working of the world. He skittered first in one direction and then in another and suddenly he was lost, forgetting where he had been, uncertain what he searched for. He dropped into the grass, the blades frilly in his face and water rising under him, and as far as he could see frothed an ocean of radiant green. There was grass and sky and the outcasts of the forest, and Jem, frightened, could not contain himself any longer: 'Kian!' he cried, lifting his voice thinly. 'Kian? Where are you?'

There was a rustle and the young cat scrabbled about to

see his sister Cally, who stepped through the grass and rubbed her cheek against his brow. He felt immediately comforted and his bearings returned to him, he recognised the trees and the path and the lie of the land. Cally walked on, toward the peppercorn, and Jem hurried after her; they stopped at the tasselled shroud of branches and looked seekingly through the weeds. They saw the quiet, shining body, saw how he did not swat the dragonfly when it dodged within reach.

The kittens raised their heads, scrutinising the field for sign of the men. They smelled the rich residue of gunshot and leather. Swallows were chikkering and dipping through the grass, and the surviving raven had returned to its leafy citadel. Cally shook the worst of the water from her before gliding into the shadows after her brother.

They crossed the paddock and arrived at the threshold of the forest, and the sun, by then, had burned off the clouds which had muffled its rays. It was the last sun of the season, and a glacial winter would pass before the skies glowed so clearly again. Jem and Cally walked without hesitation, however, into the shade – it did not occur to them to bask awhile in the weak heat or even to glance back the way they had come. They became furtive and soundless, their ears listening to the forest, their eyes dilating to its gloom. They saw the tabby stripe and the ashy flicker and followed these into a cool landscape, and out in the paddock the dragonfly was left to skate the sunshine without reason or pause.

The Wooden Forest

AT THE HEIGHT of a sultry sunburned morning a large, middle-aged cat vaulted the palings of a suburban fence and picked his rather ungainly way along the uppermost rail. The cat's coat was distinctive, black speckled on white, a pattern more commonly seen in dogs and the sole reason why the cat's owner had selected this animal, as a kitten, over his more conventionally marked littermates. The cat himself gave no thought to the uniqueness of his looks – if anything, speckling was a nuisance, for the cat frequently mistook the spots for splotches of dirt and often found himself frantically chewing at a stain that proved, in the end, to be a piece of himself. He was by nature a bad-tempered beast, prone to furballs and skin rashes as well as being insistently and incurably confrontational, and the aggravating tricks of his colouring did nothing, ever, to improve his outlook.

He reached the final fencepost and stopped with his forepaws propped on it, staring about royally. Behind him, on his own side of the fence, lay his house and garden, the tidy spread of his rightful territory. Before him, on the other side of the fence, was a territory he had recently seized as his own but which had, until the appropriation, belonged to that irritatingly lordly animal, Kian. The spotted cat had long dreamed of extending his holdings beyond the fence and his acquisition of the abutting land filled him with a leonine pride. Kian had better not think he was getting the place back.

A vehicle surged by, its bulk and speed creating a tidalwave of stuffy air that wallowed over the speckled cat and disordered his short, well-preened whiskers. Offended, the cat jumped from the fence to land doughily on the far side, where a dusty driveway followed a slight incline to the centre of the land. This driveway had always been a favoured place for the flecked cat to sun himself and he remembered how furious Kian had become whenever he spied his neighbour ensconced on its sunbathed surface, lounging about with deceptive sleepiness – deceptive, because the speckled cat's game was to wait until Kian was poised to attack before flying into the air, cackling berserkly, and vanishing at a gallop. Old Kian would almost backflip out of his skin. Swaggering like a prince along the driveway, the blotched cat's tail shimmied with satisfaction at the memory. As with all felines forced to live in uncomfortably close proximity, there had been no love lost between the spotted cat and Kian. No cat was ever so scornful as Kian, the day the speckled cat's claws were clipped; no cat was so spitefully amused as the speckled cat, when Jem and Cally arrived. The neighbours had lived in a state of rivalry, each snatching every opportunity to inflict distress upon the other. They had thefted one another's food, they had dealt each other countless thwacking blows. Once they even called a truce to hostilities as they hunched under a house together and a local mongrel snuffed and snorted at the gaps. They shared, now the spotted cat considered it, a lifetime of memories, and if cats were at all sentimental he might sit down and pass a moment in quiet regret over the loss of his sparring partner. Fortunately cats are never sentimental and although the speckled cat chose, then, to sit, this was not due to any respect for Kian. He sat because the driveway had come to an end and if he continued in that direction he would be forced to walk over chunks of shattered concrete, hazardous splintered beams, and an unstable scum of broken tiles. So the speckled cat sat, and, surveying the wasteland before him, had to concede that, while he did not in the least rue the absence of his black-and-white neighbour, there was something decidedly sinister in the fact of Kian's disappearance.

When the old woman, Ellen, disappeared, the speckled cat had become quickly aware of it; with her, he'd been enraged to discover, had gone her little car, the bonnet of which had been another of his favourite but felonious sunning positions. He had noted the arrival, soon afterward, of the large man. He had witnessed, and greatly enjoyed, the sight of Kian and the kittens unceremoniously booted from the house, the calico female crouched on the cold footpath, the black male scrabbling at the door, and Kian ignoring both of them, stalking moodily down the drive.

And that had been, as best the spotted cat could remember, the last he had seen of them, the kittens and Kian. It was peculiar. He had never heard of three cats evaporating like that. What happened next was mysterious, but not nearly so mysterious as the disappearance of those cats. If it could happen to them, the speckled cat worried, could it happen to any cat? To *him*? No, he'd decided, it could not.

After Kian had gone, the man had stayed in the house alone. One day a dog jumped the low front fence and ran around the garden, and the speckled cat, observing from a bough, had watched it track the tatters of Kian's scent over the grass and into the shrubs. The man had stormed from the house and shouted, frightening both cat and canine away.

Then, in the heavy depths of winter, the gizzards of Kian's house had been taken out. Men had arrived at the house and with them had come a colossal truck; bit by bit these men had gutted the chattels and furnishings. The speckled cat, warm behind a window, watched and was extremely interested to see a couch, a mattress, a table, many chairs, all these things bobbing and weaving down the driveway with stumpy sapien legs poking out beneath them. Bookcases, a fridge, washing baskets, potted plants; paintings and coffee-tables, cupboards and drying racks: all these items and a kaleidoscope more were carted along the driveway and pushed into the maw of the waiting truck. A piano, doorstops, photo albums, a telephone. The speckled cat had jumped into the truck and sniffed around. He'd detected, on a blanket, a trace of Kian.

When the gizzards had gone, the man went too: he and his rancid car were never seen again. Winter had lugged itself down a windswept lane. The vacant house was irresistible and the spotted cat roamed its roof, its sills, the stuffy space beneath its floor. He scratched the tree-trunks, obliterating the rents left by Kian's claws. When the cream cat who lived across the road was discovered one evening asleep on the veranda, the speckled cat had reacted with the indignation of a proprietor. It surprised him a little, how quickly he'd come to consider the territory his own. Conscious of it now, he accepted and declared his ownership with catcalls of victory. This had been a most pleasing period of the spotted cat's life. As he'd patrolled his new dominion through those short, chill, overcast days, examining every nook and strategically planting his scats everywhere, he had felt some of the hot-blooded vainglory of the young lion who slays the overlord and usurps the pride.

The days were still cool but they lasted longer, the nights left no garnish of frost on the lawn and the sun's path was taking it much higher into the sky when one morning a tribe of vehicles thundered unexpectedly into the street, titanic machines that surely had been chiselled out of stone. The spotted cat had bolted at the sight of them, burying himself in the clutter under a bed, and listened to tremendous and terrible noises that throttled the air and rose, unmistakably, from the house next door. The noise bullied into the room where he was hiding, shivering the very carpet below his feet. Only when twilight was closing and the street was quiet did he come cautiously out, too nervy to eat his waiting meal. He'd leapt to the top of the fence and stared, amazed, over his annexed domain.

The house was gone. The fence was gone. The shed was gone, and so was the garage. The shrubs were gone and the clothesline was gone. The grass was gone, and gone were all the trees. All that remained were piles of rubbish – planks and smashed bricks, broken glass and the like – and the driveway, which came to a grisly end where the garage had once been. The ground, green that morning, was a churned morass of mud. A pall of dust hung in the air and smelt old, like centuries themselves. Around the yard stood the metal monsters responsible for this astounding change of scenery, their broad treads caked with muck, their huge buckets resting on the earth but gaping, snaggle-toothed, wanting more. The cat jumped from the fence and walked through the wreckage, sniffing sceptically, tail whipping. He could not decide what he thought of all this. Cats, on the whole, dislike change. But when the moon was up, very round and small, and the stale dust had settled, he perched on a mound of rocks and rubble and concluded that he rather liked this transformation. Scrubbed and erased, the land felt cleansed. It looked like somewhere starting anew, and this suited the speckled cat. It made him feel more certain that Kian was truly gone.

A fly was circling the spotted cat and he batted it distractedly, not overly bothered by the insect but suffering, nonetheless, the compulsion to protest. That had been a good long while ago, the night he'd sat on the refuse. Since that night the weather had improved, leaves had sprouted on trees, birds had hatched another generation. Progress on the building site – for so his new territory had become, a building site, over which men sweated through the heat of each day – progress on the building site had not always been rapid, for there had been bouts of summery rain, nor trouble-free, as the frequently raised voices could testify, but a thick concrete slab had been laid and a timber frame had been erected around it and only the day previous men had monkeyed to the heights of the frame and tapped into place clanging sheets of corrugated roofing.

The driveway was becoming displeasingly warm and the flecked cat stood up smartly; he crossed the dirt to where the vast slab lay, smooth and wan as a snowdrift, yet lumpish as a dead bull. He jumped onto the slab and wandered about, stopping to inspect and ambling on. A balmy breeze twiddled his whiskers, slicking his speckled coat down, bringing with it the smell of petrol, flower fertiliser and, distinctly, milk boiling on a stove. He reared onto his hind legs and shredded an upright of the building frame. He sat back, licking his lips. He squinted over the decimated landscape, at the flat barren earth and angles. A recollection of Kian crossed his mind: whatever had happened to that cat, wherever he had gone, it was sure to be somewhere uninteresting, something absurd.

The breeze unexpectedly boiling his feline blood, the speckled cat seemed to become diabolically possessed: he threw himself down and rolled over and over, he ran around in circles and sprang bandy-legged into the air. For several moments he chased about madly, careening between the wooden studs, his tail lashing crazedly. The frenzy ceased as quickly as it began and he adopted once more the guise of a stylish animal, alert but innately calm. He prowled the slab, searching the skeletal frame. In his mind he became a wild cat, patrolling his forest home. The towering posts of the frame sprouted limbs to hide him secretively; the tin roof nailed high above became a forest's vibrant canopy, alive with scurrying prey. He heard a faint rustle and slunk immediately to the forest floor, creeping forward with exquisite care, halting when he'd slithered as near as he dared. The rustle came again and his yellow eyes blackened, the hair went prickly down his spine. His whiskers quavered as he strained his senses, his chin to the ground. There was a creature hiding somewhere in the leaf litter, some furtive forest creature filled with warm flowing fluid. The cat held his breath, his hindquarters wiggled, he awaited the perfect moment for the spring. Once more the rustle and the speckled cat propelled himself forward, an uncoiled blaze of lightning. He crashed down on his victim and sank his teeth into its neck and, tasting the sourness of weathered plastic, released the crumpled potato-chip bag he'd crushed beneath his paws.

Then came a sound which made him snap his head around, forgetting his kill instantly. It was the sound of a door opening, and he heard the clipped footsteps of his owner. The speckled cat hunkered on the concrete, determined not to move. For no good reason, he hated her. She liked to pat him, brush him, coo idiotically in his ear. She was calling him now, and his hackles rose. 'Dotty! Dotty!' she was sing-songing, her voice ludicrously trill. 'Dotty! Dotty!' He twitched a lip, revealing a fang. He would not go, he would not go. He would stay where he was, stalking through the forest. Then he heard the tumble of kibble into his bowl and suddenly, against his will, he was dashing across the slab. He was not hungry, he knew he wasn't, yet he could not resist. He clambered to the top of the fence and at its peak he wrested control of himself long enough to pause. He saw his owner, smiling at him and proffering food. He looked back at the forest, felt its dark promise of a savage world. His owner called him and he hurried to her, irresistibly compelled, but even as he slid down the fence he swore that he detested her; as he cantered across the soft summer lawn he thought of the splendid barbarous life he could be living and as he settled beside his bowl and began to eat he promised himself that one day, maybe one day very soon, he was quitting this dump, and running away.